Stories of The Sticks

Episode Two

Imperia Jobsworth is Missing

Jeanie Palfrey

HEDDON PUBLISHING

First edition published in 2021 by Heddon Publishing.

ISBN 978-1-913166-53-3

Illustrated by Jeanie Palfrey

Cover design by Catherine Clarke

This is a work of fiction. Names, characters, businesses, places, events and incidents are either the products of the author's imagination or used in a fictitious manner. Any resemblance to actual persons, living or dead, or actual events is purely coincidental.

Book design and layout by Katharine Smith, Heddon Publishing.

www.heddonpublishing.com
www.facebook.com/heddonpublishing
Twitter: @PublishHeddon

About the Author

When Jeanie was asked what she would really like to do next, she replied that she would like to write a children's book, and make models of the characters to create the illustrations from. She wasn't quite sure how that would work, but that is what popped into her head.

Having been a mature student at art college when her two children were young, gaining HND Design Modelmaking and BA(Hons) Costume for Screen and Stage, she had then immersed herself in designing and making costumes for ten years for First Position School of Dance in Bournemouth, where her children trained with Miss Natalie Pearl. But when Hattie and Lewis had both flown the nest to train as professional dancers in London, she was in need of a new direction. Hence Amy had asked that question.

So, leaving behind the costume-making, and seventeen years as Creative Artist in a day hospice, a life-changing move from Dorset to Shropshire with husband, Trev, presented her with the opportunity to do what she really wanted to do next. And she worked on a technique to achieve it:

The creation of each character begins with the written description within the story. From this, a rough sketch is drawn as a guide to making a soft sculpture model. This can then be posed and photographed, and, by drawing a grid for scale, the illustrations materialise. In *All About Stasia,* the first episode of Stories of The Sticks, the illustrations were produced entirely with a range of technical pens. For *Imperia Jobsworth is Missing*, they have been upgraded to include shading and backgrounds, inspired by an on-line course in urban sketching during lockdown!

Happily, this is still keeping her off the streets and out of trouble.

You can find out more about Jeanie, and the wonderful world of The Sticks, on Instagram:

@storiesofthesticks

To my lovely mum and dad
Monty and Stasia
who always believed in me.

And to Trev, Hattie and Lewis
who still do.

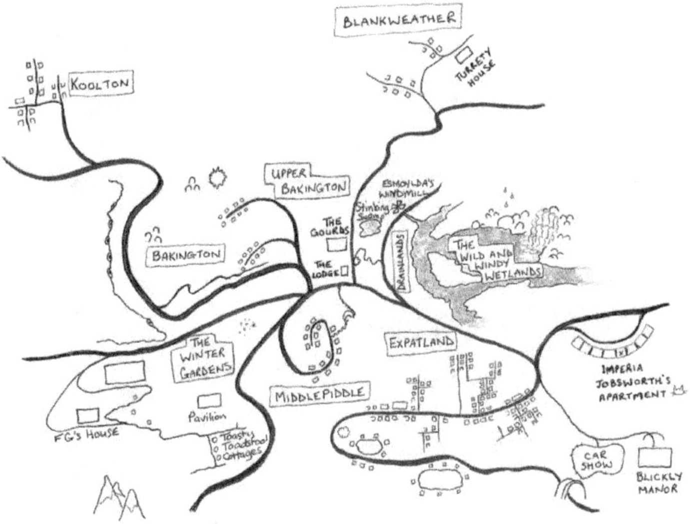
BLANKWEATHER
TURRETY HOUSE
KOOLTON
UPPER BAKINGTON
ESMOYLDA'S WINDMILL
Stinking Swamp
THE GOURDS
BAKINGTON
THE LODGE
DRAINLANDS
THE WILD AND WINDY WETLANDS
THE WINTER GARDENS
EXPATLAND
MIDDLEPIDDLE
IMPERIA JOBSWORTH'S APARTMENT
Pavilion
FG's HOUSE
Toasty Toadstool Cottages
CAR SHOW
BLICKLY MANOR

Glossary

In order of appearance:

Goblin: An ugly or grotesque creature with a tendency to be malicious. Often greedy, with a love of money. Vary in size.

Elf: A small, mischievous faerie creature, quite human in appearance, but, as with most of the rest of the faerie world creatures, with pointed ears.

Gnome: A stubborn but wise creature, practical and down-to-earth. Can be quite grumpy and disapproving of anything airy-fairy. They are stick-in-the-muds, very precise, and rather slow.

Troll: Clever creatures, who can range from a few inches to a few miles high. Very good at making things, and they like stones, bones and feathers. Often found under bridges, etc., and tend to live in small family groups, e.g. father and daughter, or mother and son. Hate lightning.

Faerie: A small human-like creature, similar to the elf in appearance, but with wings. They expect high standards from humans.

Pixie: Another mischievous creature. Finds fun in causing trouble, and at their happiest when they are being naughty. Natural gymnasts.

Boggart: A wayward, Brownie-like creature. Likes to cause annoying problems, e.g. breaking glasses, or bursting balloons.

Hob: A helpful household spirit sometimes found working in farmyards, sometimes helping in kitchens. Loves baking.

Sprite: A spiritual creature, similar to a faerie or an elf, but more ethereal.

The Gourds

Chapter One

Moving In

As she struggled to turn the key, the grinding and squealing were like fingernails scraping down a blackboard. The years of rust and grime that had built up inside the lock made entering the house a feat of real determination.

'That's the first job on the list then, Mum,' said Stasia, as the final *clunk* eventually arrived, and she turned the handle and pushed the door.

Stasia and her mum, Sarah, had been renting a cottage since they arrived in The Sticks a few months ago, having been pushed into moving there by Stasia's Uncle William. But after some exciting, though dangerous, adventures, and more importantly bonding with some of the locals, they had decided to make a permanent home there.

The decision to buy this rundown manor house that they had just entered, where a gangster goblin had lived until recently, might seem quite surprising to some. After all, the gangster and his henchmen had kidnapped Sarah, and held her hostage in their rented cottage. Stasia had managed to rescue her, though, with the help of her new friends, and also captured the goblin. Unfortunately, he had escaped, but we'll save that for later.

More importantly for now, this was the day they had got the keys for their new home, and were about to move in.

Having pushed the heavy old door open, they stood on the threshold, casting their eyes around the vast, dilapidated hallway.

'What *have* we done?!' they said together. Then they fell about laughing.

This was the first time they had seen inside the house since they had bought it, and they were looking at it with fresh eyes now that it belonged to them. It had turned out that the house had not actually belonged to Arton Mudd, and was put up for sale by the owner when Mudd was thought to be "out of the way".

'I hadn't realised quite how much work needed to be done here,' sighed Sarah, as reality dawned.

'It could be great when it's decorated, though, couldn't it?!' Stasia was bouncing up and down with excitement. 'It's amazing that we could buy somewhere like this. Even in this state!'

'True. Houses are cheaper here, but even though selling our old house has given us the money to buy it, there's not much left over to do all the work as well. We'll have to be patient, and do as much as we can by ourselves.'

And there was a lot to be done. Stasia started looking around their new home. The outside of The Gourds still looked quite impressive: double fronted, with pillars supporting the porch over the front door in the middle. The carvings around the pillars were well-worn, but they looked fine if you just squinted at them from a distance. When Stasia and Sarah had stepped up to the front door, the very first time they viewed it, they were both so excited. And even when they had seen inside, and realised it was run-down and neglected and had obviously been used as a bit of a party house, they still loved it. The wallpaper might have been hanging off the walls in shreds, and the paintwork discoloured and peeling, but it still felt like home. And so they had bought it, perhaps a bit impulsively, their hearts ruling their heads: it was a bit on the big side for the two of them. Even for the two of them and Rags. Even though she was quite large, and very hairy, and wagged her tail a lot.

'You could have one of the five bedrooms for yourself, Rags,' Sarah laughed.

'And one of the four reception rooms!' added Stasia, as she skipped into the nearest one.

The sitting room had probably been called a drawing room,

originally, as the house was very old. And many years ago, it would have been called a withdrawing room, when the gentlemen withdrew into a separate room from the ladies after dinner parties. It had obviously been impressive once, but now dust cobwebs hung dramatically from the tarnished chandelier in the centre of the remarkably high ceiling. Bits of the ceiling rose were missing, most of the bulbs had blown, and the chandelier dangled precariously at a wonky angle. The musty smell of damp and neglect was almost overpowering, but Stasia was grinning from ear to ear when she said, 'I love it here, Mum.'

'**What was that?**' Sarah shouted from a distance. '**I'm in the kitchen!**''

On hearing the word "kitchen", Rags turned tail, and bounded through the hallway, looking for Sarah. After an accidental detour into the broom cupboard, and taking a wrong turn into the downstairs water closet (toilet, to me and you), the dog eventually found the kitchen, where she raced around the table and plonked herself down in front of Sarah, looking up at her with the appealing eyes.

'I need to go shopping yet, Rags. You'll have to wait.'

Rags grumbled as she slumped down on the yet-to-be-scrubbed kitchen floor. Meanwhile, Stasia had gone out through the French doors onto the terrace, back through another set of doors into a different room, then, leaving by yet another door, found herself in a hidden part of the hallway, which she had never even seen before.

'**This hallway is enormous!**' she shouted.

'**You don't have to shout!**' shouted Sarah, laughing as they came face-to-face, rounding a pillar. 'The furniture should be arriving soon. Uncle William arranged for it to be delivered today. Shall we start cleaning, so that we can bring our stuff in out of the car? Is Drivel still out there?'

'I thought he was in my bag when we came in,' said Stasia, sure that her unsuitably named Helpful Elf had taken up his usual position, so that she ended up carrying him everywhere. Lazy Elf might have been more apt. 'Although I'm not sure where I left it.'

'Your bag is in the kitchen, but Rags was lying on it, so I hope he's not still in it?!'

Horrified at that thought, Stasia charged through the hallway, raced past the open fireplace, leapt over a pile of rubbish, and skidded into the kitchen.

'Rags, Rags, get up! Are you ok, Drivel? Oh, Drivel, I'm really sorry, I didn't realise I'd left it on the floor. Drivel! Rags, get up!' Stasia pulled on Rags' collar to get her to her feet. Drivel might be a miserable companion, but she was responsible for him. And she had even grown quite fond of him.

'Drivel?!!!' She pulled her bag wide open. Not an elf to be seen. **'Drivel!!!!'**

There was a faint banging somewhere upstairs. Stasia sprinted up the long, shallow staircase, listening out for any reply. Reaching the sprawling galleried landing, she called his name again. Sarah caught up with her just as the banging restarted, but it was louder this time.

'It seems to be coming from that room, there.' Sarah pointed along the landing.

'Where does that lead? I don't remember that one.'

'Actually, neither do I.'

As the banging continued, Sarah crept cautiously towards the door. Taking hold of the handle, she quietly called out Drivel's name again, and a loud ***bang*** came from inside. She looked at Stasia.

'It must be him, mustn't it?'

'Yeah. Must be.'

Sarah pressed down on the lever and jumped, as the door unexpectedly swung towards her. As it opened fully, she realised that it wasn't a room at all. It was a large, walk-in cupboard.

'Ooh!' she exclaimed.

'What?'

'Great storage.'

'Never mind that,' said Stasia. 'Is Drivel there?'

'**Yes**!' shouted a very grumpy elf. He appeared from behind the open door, his leafy shirt and trousers festooned with cobwebs, and his hat playing host to a posse of spiders. They decided not to mention that to him, as it would only have made matters worse.

'Are you ok?' asked Stasia, trying not to giggle.

'*No*!' he grumbled. 'I've been stuck in that cupboard for two and a half months.'

'We've only been here half an hour.'

Sarah was more sympathetic. 'I suppose you couldn't reach the door handle to get out. Why didn't you climb up on those boxes?'

'**I did climb up on those boxes**! **I'm not stupid**! The door wouldn't open! It was stuck!'

'Oh dear, we'll put that on the list, too.'

'I'll try it,' said Stasia.

'Why, don't you believe me?' Drivel was deeply offended.

'I just thought I might be able to see what went wrong.'

Stasia stepped into the cupboard and closed the door. Drivel smirked, presuming Stasia would get stuck too, but the smile soon melted away, when she casually opened the door again and stepped out.

'Cross it off your list, Mum.'

☆

After three hours of cleaning, scrubbing, dusting, and disposing of debris, Stasia and Sarah collapsed in a heap. The furniture had arrived, but the gnomes who delivered it had just left it in the driveway, and driven off. Apparently, Uncle William had paid for delivery only, and they were told in no uncertain terms by the delivery gnomes that they were lucky they were even unloading it from the truck for them.

'"Delivery only" means delivery *only*, see? Lucky for you that you got *us* today. If you had got Algy and Peat, you'd have had to unload it yourselves, while they sat and had a cup of tea. Mind you, we might not be so accommodating next time. "Delivery only" means *delivery only*. See?'

And off they went.

'What's for dinner, Mum? I'm starving.'

'Well, my lovely, I'm afraid the cupboard is bare. Clean, now, but completely bare. Luckily, we have an invitation for dinner, don't we?'

'Oh yes, from Dorissa and Snooch. Can't help worrying about

what dinner might be, though. I still remember the cup of tea with the spoon standing up in middle, it was so thick. And the colour!'

'Well, now we're living here in The Sticks, I suppose we'll have to be open-minded about things like food. We could start growing our own vegetables, though. Maybe we could ask Clive about that.'

'Well, Esmoylda said she would come over to help tomorrow, so we can talk about that then.'

Before they moved to The Sticks, Stasia would never in her wildest dreams have thought she would become best friends with a troll. Not least because she had never met one before. But Esmoylda had turned out to be the best friend anyone could wish for. And her dad, Clive, was always happy to help, and the best handyman ever. Perhaps that should be handytroll.

He and Esmoylda lived separately from Esmoylda's mum and brother, because that was the way that trolls had lived for hundreds of years. Esmoylda had been planning to talk to her dad about it. As Stasia's dad had died over two years ago, and she still missed him, she agreed that it seemed wrong that Esmoylda should lose her mum when she could still be with her, just because of an age-old custom.

Dorissa and Snooch had become friends of theirs, too. The faerie brother and sister had been struggling to run a detective agency from The Lodge, by the entrance to The Gourds. Now that Sarah and Stasia had bought The Gourds, The Lodge had come as part of the package, and Sarah was considering taking on the organisation of the agency, just until they could get someone else to do it. The siblings certainly did need help, especially now that the Law Keepers were mainly based in Expatland. Sarah would never have imagined herself running so much as a coffee morning, never mind something like a detective agency, before coming here. She wouldn't have had the confidence to do it. Things that had happened in the first few weeks of living in the world-next-door had started to make a difference to that.

Chapter Two

The Dinner Party

'That was a lovely meal, thank you both.' Sarah was being polite, but she had arranged her knife and fork carefully, to hide the remains of the food that she couldn't force herself to eat.

Stasia nudged her mum under the table and grinned at her with widened eyes. 'You've always taught me not to lie!' she whispered.

'Who, me? I said *that*?! Well, I'm sure I must have added that there are times when it's only polite to do so.' Sarah winked at her daughter.

'Glad you liked it.' Snooch was beaming. 'It was our mum's recipe. Although I'm not sure I boiled the…'

'I'm sure you boiled them long enough, Snooch,' interrupted Dorissa, 'but don't give away the secret ingredients. Anyone not used to our unique cuisine might be put off.'

'But everyone likes boiled…'

'Snooch!'

Sarah and Stasia looked at each other, wondering what they had just eaten. Perhaps it was better that they didn't know.

'Anyway,' said Dorissa, 'I'm guessing you didn't accept our invitation just to sample our culinary delights? Have you decided what you're going to do with us? Are you going to throw us out onto the streets?'

She pulled her saddest face, with puppy dog eyes.

'Umm… no, I… why, do you want to leave, then? I thought perhaps…'

Stasia whispered to her mum. 'Confident and positive? Didn't you say that was how you were going to be from now on?'

Sarah nodded and cleared her throat. **'No!"** she accidentally shouted.

Laughing at Sarah's unexpected response, Dorissa got up, and started collecting the dinner plates around the table. **'OK!'** she shouted back, with a relieved smirk. 'So, what *is* the plan?'

Sarah sat up straight, folded her hands in front of her, and rested them on the table - avoiding the splinters. Stasia watched her mum proudly, as she steeled herself to take charge - probably for the first time ever in her life.

'With your agreement, I'm taking over the running of the detective agency, until we can find someone more suitable to do it.' Sarah let out a long sigh of relief after making such a bold statement. She added, 'We thought perhaps Faerie Godmother would be a good choice to take over eventually, if she agrees?'

'Super,' said Snooch.

'Great,' said Dorissa, wiping her hands on her skirt as she returned from the kitchen. She sat down next to her brother, upright and alert, determined to show she was paying attention. Snooch was absentmindedly playing an illogical version of tiddlywinks with the coasters. Stasia gave him a nudge just before Sarah threw a screwed-up napkin at him, playfully shouting, 'But I will need all the help I can get, to make it work!'

'Who from?' asked Snooch, looking up just in time to get the full force of the missile in his face.

'From whom!' Drivel interjected. He liked to score points.

'Us, hopefully?' said Dorissa.

'Of course,' said Sarah. 'It was you two that started the agency in the first place.'

'I'll be helping!' said Stasia.

'Yes, but you must fit it in around your schoolwork, my lovely. The home-school lesson plans should arrive soon.'

Stasia sighed.

'Me, too!' Drivel was determined not to be forgotten in the plans for the new agency. Being a detective was what he had always dreamt of doing, apparently. He had formed his napkin into a version of Dorissa's deerstalker, and was wearing it with pride.

'I could help in the office and talk to...'

'No, Snooch,' corrected Dorissa, '*I* could work in the office, and organise...'

'NO!!'

They fell silent and turned slowly towards Sarah. She *was* taking charge. Moving to The Sticks was definitely having a positive effect on her. And sitting there, surrounded by the peculiar paraphernalia that Dorissa and Snooch had gathered over the years, Sarah and Stasia seemed surprisingly at ease. Not like the first time Stasia had visited The Lodge, unnerved by the dramatic doorbell, and the thick faerie tea. Now it seemed that they found it all more familiar, and the fact that the shelves were wonky-donkey, and the cupboards misshapen and lopsided, just added to its charm.

'No,' Sarah was saying. '*I* will work in the office, take the enquiries, and give the orders.'

'Go, Mum,' cheered Stasia proudly.

'And Esmoylda is going to help, too. She talks more sense than the lot of you put together.'

'Ouch.' Dorissa was hurt.

'True,' Snooch agreed.

'But... but...' Drivel couldn't justify an argument.

'So, what are we doing first?' asked Stasia, hopeful that schoolwork might get forgotten.

'Well, I've spoken to the Law Keepers' new office in Expatland, and they are asking all local agencies to help find Arton Mudd.

And as we know him better than some, they are hoping we can come up with some leads. Apparently, he's wanted for a number of crimes, not just what he did to us.'

'I could come over tomorrow…' Dorissa started.

'Ooh, and me…' Snooch joined in.

'And what about…'

Before Drivel could finish, Sarah put her hands over her ears, and started singing to herself. And then she shouted again.

'**Right!** Let's just think for a minute. How shall we go about finding Arton Mudd? Where would he go? Who would he get help from?'

'I know!' Drivel put his hand in the air, as if he were at school. 'Rizber and Razber! Mudd's henchmen.'

'Yes, but they're locked up, aren't they?' said Stasia. 'It was only Arton Mudd who escaped.'

Drivel sulked.

'Yeah,' agreed Snooch. 'I did see them the other day, though.'

They all turned slowly to look at Snooch.

'You saw them?' asked Dorissa. 'And you never thought to mention it?'

'Mention what?' asked Snooch.

'You are *sure* it was them?' asked Stasia.

'Big goblins? Riding motorbikes? Dressed in leather, with cowboy hats?'

'That was them,' they chorused.

'So, they are free, too,' said Sarah. 'The Law Keepers' office didn't mention them, though, so they must have let them go.'

'You were right, then, Drivel.' Stasia patted him on the back so hard he fell off his chair. 'Riz and Raz *would* be the ones that Mudd would go to for help. They'll do anything for him. If we find *them*, we'll find Arton Mudd. Sorted!'

'You make it sound very easy, my lovely,' said Sarah. 'But actually, do we even know where to start looking for Riz and Raz? Where do they live? Who do they live with?'

'What did they have for breakfast?' Snooch thought he was being helpful.

'Goblins used to live around the Bakington area, mainly,' said Dorissa, ignoring her brother, 'in the cave houses, until Mudd diverted the water system to his new development. I heard they had to move out and head towards Koolton.'

'And in Middlepiddle,' added Stasia. 'That's where I first met Garf and Nostrils, wasn't it, Drivel?!'

Drivel mumbled something and looked guilty, remembering he had led Stasia into some difficult and dangerous situations when he had been her Helpful Elf. When she first arrived in The Sticks, she had gone to collect him from the very scary Elf Services Administrator, by whom he had been shut inside a shabby little house-box. Thinking about it now, Stasia wasn't surprised at Drivel being so grumpy. Who wouldn't be? Kept in a box in a cupboard with only that horrible administrator for company! But now he was the first to admit, much to Stasia's relief, that after leading them both into a succession of disastrous situations, he was just not cut out for the job.

'So, perhaps it's a case of making door-to-door enquiries first, then? Until we get a lead?' Sarah was making notes as she spoke. 'Anyone who has seen Riz and Raz around would certainly remember them, and might be glad to tell us what they know.'

'Ok,' said Dorissa, straightening the layers of frilly net on her skirt. 'Sounds like you're going to be busy. Let us know when you want us to help with something.' She leant back on the sofa and stretched lazily. Snooch was already dozing next to her.

'Thank you,' said Sarah. 'I will. I would like you and Snooch to get up early tomorrow morning and start the door-to-door enquiries, until you find out where Rizber and Razber live. Then bring any information you receive back to me. Thank you for a lovely evening. Goodnight.'

Stasia got up quickly and scooped Drivel into her bag, following her mum out of the front door, down the well-worn steps, and along the path to the gate. Looking back to wave goodbye, she saw the bemused faerie faces at the front door, trying to raise a smile. Her mum was quietly giggling to herself.

'They weren't expecting that, were they?!' said Stasia. 'Confident and positive, Mum!'

By the time they were out of earshot, Sarah was laughing out loud. 'No. I don't think they're used to working hard at all, which is why the agency was never a success. Do you remember when they said that no one seemed to want to give them any work? I think we know why, now, don't we! But if they want to stay in the lodge, they'll have to work for it.'

'You're a hard woman,' laughed Stasia.

Chapter Three

Start of the Investigations

Stasia and Sarah didn't see the siblings again until the following afternoon. They turned up at the door of The Gourds, looking exhausted, and feeling sorry for themselves.

'Come in, sit down, put your feet up.' Sarah was trying hard not to laugh as she showed them into the sitting room. They had to pick their way through the dust and the damp, musty wallpaper strewn on the floor.

'I'm pooped,' sighed Snooch, flopping onto the sofa and

putting his feet up on a tin of Marginally Mauve Eggshell. Dorissa joined him, touching her brow dramatically, after first carefully removing the wallpaper stripper so she could sit down safely.

'Well?' Stasia asked. 'Did you find them?'

'Find who?' Snooch had already forgotten what they'd been doing.

'No,' said Dorissa, 'but after *extensive, exhausting* house-to-house enquiries, we managed to find their parents.'

'Whose parents?' asked Snooch.

'Riz's and Raz's! You know that!' Dorissa's exasperation with her brother had to spill out occasionally.

'Oh,' he replied. 'That's who they were.'

'Great,' said Sarah. 'What did you find out?'

'Well,' began Dorissa, 'first of all, we found Rizber's parents. They weren't too sure about talking to us, until I told them that we went to school with Riz.'

'Oh yeah,' said Snooch. 'I remember you saying that. I didn't know we were at school with him. I must have forgotten.'

'That's because we weren't.'

'But you said we were?!'

'I know! So they would talk to us!'

'You told a lie!'

'Not exactly. We are about the same age. We were at school at the same time. Therefore... we were at school with him... timewise... just... not at the same school.'

'So, anyway,' interrupted Sarah, 'what did they say? Did you find out where they were? Had they seen Arton Mudd?'

'*Well,*' began Dorissa, a little more dramatically this time, 'as soon as we mentioned Mudd's name, Mrs Rizber was *off.* Apparently, he went to school with both Rizber and Razber. And Mrs Rizber had a whole lot to say about how her little angel was led astray by *that Razber creature,* who seemed to be *determined* to drag him along when he was following *that Mudd* like a lap goblin. Her little Rizzy would not have *dreamt* of going off the straight and narrow if it hadn't been for *him.* According to her. And as for *that Arton Mudd! Who does he think he is?* She kept repeating that.'

'I wondered why she kept asking that,' Snooch muttered. 'He must know who he is, doesn't he? Wouldn't his mum have told him?'

'No love lost between Riz's mum and the Razber family, then.' Sarah made a note of that.

'None,' Dorissa agreed. 'You'd think they were still kids, the way she was talking. As if they were still at school.'

'Did you find out where they are?' asked Sarah.

'*Well,*' Dorissa began again, with another dramatic flourish, 'Mrs Rizber told us where to find the Razbers.'

'They were next door,' said Snooch. 'Quite easy to find.'

'So we went next door and spoke to Razber's mum,' continued Dorissa.

'She offered us a cup of tea.'

'She did. After she heard that we'd been at her neighbour's.'

'Trying to outdo the Rizbers, by the sound of it,' said Sarah.

'Oh,' said Snooch, 'I thought she was just being nice.'

'She told us that her little Razzy had always been a good little goblin until *that nasty Arton Mudd* came to the school,' Dorissa went on. 'And young Rizber wasn't much better, she kept saying. She said he was a bad influence on their precious *Razzywazzy*.'

Everyone cringed.

'So, each family blames the other one,' said Stasia. 'They've held on to that grudge for years, haven't they!'

'But did you find out where they were? Especially Arton Mudd?' asked Sarah.

Dorissa and Snooch looked at each other. Then back at Sarah. They answered together.

'We forgot to ask.'

✡

'I could do without this, really,' said Sarah. 'I hoped that I could just do some admin for the agency, not do *their* work as well!'

'I could go back to Koolton with Esmoylda, to find out where they are,' offered Stasia, 'then you can stay here and try and sort them out.'

'That's a tall order.'

'Also, you know we thought maybe Faerie Godmother might be a good one to take charge? Well, Esmoylda said that Clive sent FG a sycamore seed message to put the idea to her. She'll be here soon, so we can ask her.'

'Faerie Godmother is coming here?'

'No. Esmoylda!'

'Thank goodness for that. Look at the state of the place!'

The creepy sound of the rusty old door-knocker resounded

through the house. Stasia answered the door to her best friend.

'I just saw Dorissa and Snooch heading for home,' Esmoylda said as she wiped her bare feet on the dustsheet in the hall. 'Did they find out where Arton Mudd is? Or Riz and Raz?'

'Hmmm,' said Stasia, closing the door. 'The short answer is "no". I'll fill you in on the rest later. Come on through. Mind the dust extractor.'

They joined Sarah in the sitting room, where she was half hidden by a sheet of wallpaper that was coming off the wall almost completely intact.

'This is so satisfying!' she exclaimed, as she climbed out from under it. 'Hello, Esmoylda. Good to see you. Have you heard what happened this morning? Those two are going to drive me mad. Stasia said your dad got in touch with FG. Any news? Please say yes!'

'Yes, Dad got an answer back, but, apparently, she's got a lot on at the moment. She didn't say what, but she did say she would give it some thought.'

'I'll keep everything crossed for now, then,' said Sarah, crossing everything. 'In the meantime, would you mind going with Stasia to retrace Dorissa and Snooch's steps from this morning? And do what they were supposed to do!'

'Look out!' shouted Stasia.

Everyone ducked. But, as Drivel had chosen that particular moment to enter the room, he received the full force of the loaded sycamore seed, which had flown in through the open window. Staggering backwards across the room, he tripped into a bowl of dirty water.

'Well done, Drivel, you caught it,' Stasia giggled.

Drivel made an indescribable noise, chucked the seed on the floor, and clambered out of the bowl.

'You kept it dry, too!' she called after him, as he dripped out of the room.

'Oh dear,' said Esmoylda.

'He'll be alright,' said Stasia. 'Loves a bit of drama.'

Sarah had picked up the loaded seed. She was getting used to the communication system now, and knew that these contained a voicemail message, rather than just a written one. She wished there were a less aggressive delivery method, though. 'What would have happened if the window had been closed?' She shook her head.

Setting it down on the table, Sarah pulled the wings downwards, until she heard a click to start the message.

"Hello? Hello?

Ooh, I don't know what to say. It's just very dismaying!

Help me, please. Can you help? You see, my daughter is missing. I phoned her office to have a talk with her, and I was told she hasn't been in for days!! So I had a cup of tea. But why didn't she tell me? I'm her mother! It's all too much.

I think we've got a crisis on our hands!!"

'Well, another case already!' exclaimed Stasia, 'and we haven't even got started on the first one yet. No name or contact details, though. How are we supposed to... *ouch!*'

A second missile hit her on the back of the head. Rubbing it with one hand, she passed the second seed to Sarah, who repeated the process:

"It's me again. I forgot to say, it's Muriel Jobsworth, Turrety House, Blankweather.

Please come now!!"

'It sounds urgent,' said Sarah. 'A missing daughter is more urgent than a missing gangster, isn't it? You two go to Blankweather, and speak to this Muriel Jobsworth, if you don't mind, and I'll send the terrible twins back to Koolton. Let's see if they can do the job right this time.'

'Ok,' said Stasia. 'I doubt Drivel will be coming with us, though. I think he's still sulking somewhere.'

She grabbed her bag and headed for the door.

'What do I need for Blankweather? I haven't been there. Is it cold? Hot? Wet?'

'It's nothing,' came a little voice from inside her bag. 'It's blank weather. That's why it's called...'

'Blankweather!' finished Stasia, nodding.

'Well done,' said the voice, sarcastically. 'Now, can we get on and do something before I die of boredom?'

'Yes, Drivel,' said Stasia.

And with Rags squeezing through the door as soon as it opened, determined not to be left behind, the foursome set off on their very own mission.

Chapter Four

Muriel's House

Blankweather lived up to its name. There was a general feeling of nothingness about it. No sun. No rain. No wind. No snow, hail, sleet… Nothing. It was even hard to guess what the temperature might be, or even which season it was. The trees and shrubs were all evergreens, and there wasn't a single flower to be seen. Just bland, really. Blank, in fact. Turrety House was quite easy to find, though. It had a turret right in the middle of the house, at the front. Esmoylda knocked on the door, as professionally as she could.

'Hello?' said someone who did not appear to be expecting

anybody. She did sound like the voice on the message, though.

'We are here in response to your message to the Detective Agency,' said Esmoylda, continuing the professional air.

The door opened. 'Oh yes, yes, come in. I'm sorry, I'm just not myself today.'

The little elfin-like Muriel led them into the house, across the vast, tiled floor in the hallway, and up the stairs, to a sprawling sitting room. The far-reaching views from the arched windows were of nothing in particular. Like the weather. As Muriel sat on a chair in the corner, she looked a little lost in her own house.

'I'm overwrought,' she declared. 'I'll make a cup of tea for us, shall I?'

'No,' said Stasia, a little too quickly, not being a lover of faerie tea. 'Just tell us how we can help.'

'I don't know where to start…'

'Just take a deep breath,' Esmoylda said, helpfully.

'It takes more than deep breaths when you're about to explode!!'

Esmoylda and Stasia were a little taken aback by such a dramatic response, so they sat on the nearest sofa, and waited quietly.

'It's Imperia, you see,' began Muriel, calming down and getting up. As she paced the room, Rags followed. 'She's rather volcanic sometimes, is Imperia. And now she's missing.'

Imperia Jobsworth. That name started to ring a bell with Stasia. 'How old is she?' she asked.

Muriel looked horrified. 'I beg your *pardon!* I can't tell you that! She would never forgive me!'

'Does she live with you?' Esmoylda asked.

'Does that matter?'

'Is she a child?' Stasia persisted, bluntly.

'A child? *A child?* Who said she was a child?'

'Where does Imperia live?' Esmoylda tried again.

'She has an apartment on the outskirts of Expatland. A marvellous apartment. Hobnobbing with the elite there, she is, according to Imperia. She is on the executive pension scheme, too, you know…'

'Where does she work?' interrupted Stasia.

'In the Helpful Elf department of the Natural Elf Service. She's an Elf Services Administrator.'

Stasia and Drivel audibly drew breath at the same time, as they realised they knew exactly who Imperia Jobsworth was. Esmoylda, having guessed the significance, took over the questioning.

'Have you reported her missing to the Law Keepers, Muriel?'

'I did, as a matter of fact, yes. But they were about as much use as a flat fish fan. They said she had probably just gone for a bargain break in Bakington, or a weekend in the Wet and Windys. Does that sound likely to you? They thought they were being witty and clever. There is nothing clever about them, whatsoever. They wouldn't listen when I told them she would not just up and leave without a word. They said anything is possible. I said it is possible that goblins knit their own winter undergarments, but that doesn't often happen, either. Fortunately. She might go for a brisk walk occasionally, without informing anyone, but that is about the extent of it. So, I left it for about a week. I kept going back to her apartment, to see if she had returned, and to feed the kattles, when I realised that she had definitely not been home. My mind has been well and truly engaged, trying to think where she could have gone. And you don't just jump at the first idea. There are a lot of possibilities to consider.'

'So, what did you do next?' Esmoylda tried to get Muriel back on track.

'I went back to the Law Keepers, of course! I thought they would take it more seriously when a whole week had gone by with no news. But all they are capable of is small-mindedness, nastiness, and provocation. They told me it was even less serious after a week, because if anything had happened to her, I would have heard by now!!!! How did they expect me to react to that?! Why were they surprised when I threw my shopping at them? And how was I supposed to have remembered, in a time of enlarged exasperation, that I had been to Malvolia Myddle's trifle shop that morning. Pumpkin and mingleberry trifle leaves a permanent stain on Law Keepers' uniforms, apparently. My case comes up next week.'

'Oh dear,' said Esmoylda, sheepishly, 'I think that might have been one of my dad's. He supplies to Malvolia Myddle. I had better let him know about the staining.'

(Esmoylda's father, Clive, grew pumpkins all year round, and made them into concoctions with all different combinations of fruits. Some more successful than others.)

There might have been some logic in what the Law Keepers had said, but that wouldn't stop a mother from worrying. Even though the missing daughter was definitely not a child. Nor was she someone who many people would think needed looking after.

Imperia Jobsworth was the formidable official Stasia had gone to see when she first arrived in The Sticks. The one that gave her

Drivel to act as a Helpful Elf (and who had locked him in that box for so long). But Stasia knew that she needed to be professional and so kept her personal feelings to herself. She stayed quiet, and let Esmoylda talk to Muriel.

'Would you like us to go over to Imperia's apartment tomorrow, and see if there is anything there to give us a clue to her whereabouts?'

Stasia and Drivel were extremely impressed with her wording.

'I think that would be eminently suitable,' replied Muriel. Her wording was extraordinary, but it takes all sorts.

'I think she means yes,' said Drivel.

Chapter Five

Imperia's Apartment

After a short, bumpy train ride, the party approached the apartment where Imperia lived. It was on the second floor of one of the terraced buildings that formed an impressive crescent on the outskirts of Expatland.

They entered the communal hall and climbed the stairs, glancing through the windows as they went, to see glimpses of the gardens behind the apartments. Probably not the kind of place that people would imagine Imperia Jobsworth living. It was quiet, and welcoming… and she most certainly wasn't.

On reaching the second floor, Muriel paused and leant against the wall on the long landing, gasping for breath. When she was able to speak, she wheezed: 'Honestly, why did she choose to live on the second floor of a building with no lift? She is so stubborn! You have no idea what I have to put up with! I told her! I told her to get something on the ground floor, with doors opening onto the garden, and no stairs to deal with. I give her excellent advice, and this is the thanks I get, for Heaven's sake. Stairs! Stairs! And more stairs! According to Imperia, as a solitary single, she is *safer* up here. As if she's some silly woman that needs protecting! But then… oh… oh, no. Perhaps she was right? But living up here didn't keep her safe after all, did it?! There is a very real prospect that she was right, after all….'

Changing the subject for a moment, to keep Muriel calm, Esmoylda gently asked her why she hadn't used her wings to fly up the stairs.

'Oh, I couldn't do that,' exclaimed Muriel. 'Imperia wouldn't like that at all. She doesn't like anyone to know that we are of elfin family. She feels that she would lose respect in her place of employment if anyone thought she was related to the elves she dished out to the incomers.'

Drivel popped his head up out of Stasia's bag, indignant. 'And what would be so terrible about that?!'

'Oh, hello Drivel,' said Muriel, surprised. 'How's your mum?'

Stasia was about to inquire as to whether 'incomers' was a derogatory term, when the first door on the landing opened, and then another, and another. Each of the occupants stepped out onto the landing, to find out what was going on. Two faeries, and a noticeably diminutive troll.

The first faerie was in a glamorous dressing gown and face-pack, with her hair wrapped up in a pink fluffy towel. 'Oh, hello, Muriel. Is this about your Imperia doing a flit?'

'I heard about that,' said the second, attired in a frilly apron over expensive-looking exercise kit. She held a broom in one hand, and a feather duster in the other. 'I was reading an article in a magazine in the hairdresser's the other day. Apparently, *thousands* walk out of their homes every year. Never to be heard of again!'

Muriel gasped, and visibly slumped at the knees.

'I'm sure it's more common than we realise,' said the first, oblivious to Muriel's distress, and struggling to speak without cracking the mud. 'Mostly 'cos they can't stand it anymore, and want a new life.'

'Actually, it's quite an attractive proposition – wipe the slate clean and start again. Change your name!' She flicked the duster.

'Maybe we should all try it,' called the troll from down the corridor. She was dressed in a smart suit, with a briefcase by her feet. 'Reinvent ourselves.'

'Actually, no. I don't think I would change a thing,' said the face-pack faerie.

'Well, I think that shows a complete lack of imagination. If she has gone and done it, I admire her for it,' said the second faerie, with a sweep of the broom.

'What about her friends, Muriel?' asked the business-like troll, being more helpful.

'I just don't really know,' cried Muriel. 'The longer it goes on, the more worried I am. I can't believe she wouldn't contact anybody.' Sobbing, she fumbled for her key, and opened the door between Duster Faerie and Business Troll.

As Stasia went to follow Muriel and Esmoylda into the apartment, the troll waved her hand to attract her attention. She told Stasia that she worked in the same department as Imperia, and they were having a promotion stall at the Festival of Transport in Expatland this weekend, if they needed to talk to her work colleagues.

Stasia thanked her, but then, as she was closing the door, she heard Face-pack saying, 'That Muriel, she makes an art form of falling to pieces.'

'I thought she was looking a bit frayed around the edges,' replied Duster.

Inside the apartment, Stasia passed Muriel, who was flaked out on the sofa, and made her way over to Esmoylda. 'Do you think Imperia has got any friends?'

'I was wondering that. No one seems to have mentioned any, so far.'

'I'll leave you to look around,' said Muriel, as she forced herself off the sofa, dramatically. 'I've got to feed the kattles. Goodness knows what Imperia was thinking of, going off without asking anyone to feed them. But she hasn't just gone off, has she?! She must have been kidnapped or something!! She wouldn't have left them on their own! She wouldn't have gone away without telling me! She would have asked me to feed them!!! Oh, thank goodness I came looking for her before they all starved to death!!!!!!!!' She fled to the kitchen.

Imagining a herd of cows sitting at the kitchen table, cutlery poised and waiting for dinner, Stasia poked her head round the door. She was relieved to see Muriel feeding two small cat-like creatures, with long pointy ears.

'This is Lorry and Hardel,' said Muriel, stroking their heads. Their purring was as loud as a dog's bark.

Back in the sitting room, Stasia joined Esmoylda in methodically searching through drawers and cupboards. They even took a look up the chimney, trying to find any clue to Imperia's disappearance.

'It feels wrong, looking through someone's private things,' said Esmoylda, 'even though we've been asked to. What if she walked in now and caught us!'

'That's a scary thought,' Stasia agreed, 'and I don't even know what we're looking for!'

'Nor me, but I'm hoping we'll know it when we find it. There isn't much in here. No letters or notes or anything. I wonder what's through this door.'

The next room looked instantly more promising. It was a study-come-library, with shelves full of books and papers. The desk under the window was similar to the one in Imperia's office, where

Stasia first met her. Piles of paperwork. Paper clips, bull clips, biscuits, make-up…

'Make-up?!' Stasia couldn't contain her surprise.

'That's unexpected,' agreed Esmoylda, 'from all that you've said about her. But this is strange-looking stuff. Nothing like my mum would use.'

'Oh,' said Stasia, taking a closer look. 'I've seen some like that when my dad played the dame in the village hall panto one year. It's theatrical make-up, I think. Really thick and greasy. Yuck!' She wiped it off her finger onto her jeans.

'Panto? What's that?'

'When a man dresses as a woman, and a girl dresses as a man. I'll explain some other time.'

Esmoylda was already concentrating on something else. She had picked up a photograph from the desk. 'I could swear this is FG,' she said, surprised.

'It certainly is,' agreed Stasia.

'And look here. This could be FG's address on the back. It is in The Winter Gardens. Why would she want that? And a date. A few days ago. And "300", next to that.'

'Let me see!' Drivel shuffled in from another room, apparently wearing Imperia's shoes. 'FG had a big party that day. My cousin Hoogoo told me. I didn't go, because I was helping you pack, ready to move to your new house.' Perhaps Stasia was going to ask him to define "help" at this point, but decided not to stem the flow of information, in case it was useful. 'It was for her 300th birthday!'

'Is Imperia a friend of FG's, then?' asked Esmoylda.

'Of course not.' Drivel seemed to take that idea as a personal insult.

That last remark was almost drowned out by a loud noise out in the road, below Imperia's window. They ran across the room, each tripping over Rags on the way, as she tried to work out which way to run, and why. As they reached the window, they collectively drew in a sharp breath. There were Rizber and Razber on their motorbikes, looking up at the window. When they saw Esmoylda and Stasia, they took off down the road. Muriel came out of the kitchen to see what the noise was.

'Does Imperia know Rizber and Razber?' asked Esmoylda.

'Who?' replied Muriel.

'Does she know FG?'

'FG?'

'Faerie Godmother.'

'Everyone knows Faerie Godmother.'

'Personally?' asked Esmoylda. 'Well enough to be invited to her party?'

'Imperia is very important, you know. It is quite possible. Although I would have thought she would have mentioned it to me.'

'And is she involved with acting on stage, at all?' asked Stasia.

'Don't be ridiculous.'

'Well, she does have some stage make-up here,' said Esmoylda.

'And make-up wipes?' asked Muriel.

'No, I couldn't see any.'

'Well, there you are, then. She must be alright, after all. She must have planned to leave. Nobody would just flee into the night remembering to take their make-up wipes.'

Chapter Six

An Interesting Journey

The journey to Faerie Godmother's house was interesting. Having realised that the only course of action next was to go and see FG, Esmoylda had suggested Muriel go home and try not to worry. She assured her that she and Stasia would go to The Winter Gardens the following day, to find out if anyone had seen Imperia there. As they needed to get there as quickly as possible, Esmoylda had suggested that they borrow a cart from Clive. So she turned up at The Gourds the next morning to pick Stasia up, in a vehicle the like of which had never been seen before. Which was probably just as well.

The pedal-powered cabriolet was created entirely from recycled plastic. Well, reused, rather than recycled. You could still recognise what each item was, if you looked closely, and in many of the containers the remains of the original contents were all too obvious. Some were green and furry, and a bit smelly. Somehow, it all held together with rubber bands, string, and something that looked suspiciously liked chewing gum. It reminded Stasia of somebody her dad had talked about. Heath Robinson had been known for his pictures of outrageously complicated designs to accomplish the simplest of tasks. She thought he would have loved this. Her dad would have, too.

The windscreen might have once been the side of a fish tank, with the irrigation tubing still attached. The steering wheel was a nasty neon hula hoop, and the seats were semi-deflated space hoppers. Two pairs of perished divers' flippers formed the pedals, attached to a wobbly mechanism of plumbing pipework that linked both the driver's and the passenger's together, so that they could pedal in synchronicity. The controls on the dashboard (a series of labelled Tupperware lids, with lifetime guarantees) were a mixture of red, blue and green milk bottle tops, overcoat buttons, duffle coat toggles, and toothpaste tops. A framework of hosepipe draped with fertiliser bags formed the body (visually declaring the advantages of compost for your camellias). The chassis was the aforementioned variety of mouldy containers, and at least ten green water bottles, firmly welded together with the stuff that looked suspiciously like chewing gum. The wheels were unopened economy-size tubs of emulsion paint, containing *Can't Cope Blue, Bellow Yellow, Pond Slime Green,* and *Pretty in Puce.*

'This is quite amazing,' declared Stasia, either in admiration or in horror.

'You don't have to be polite,' said Esmoylda. 'This was Dad's mock-up. He's built the real one now, and is going to enter it into the competition at the Transport Festival in Expatland. We wouldn't be able to reach the pedals on that one, though, so this is all we've got. Shall we try it?'

'Of course,' said Stasia, trying to work out how to get into the passenger seat, especially as she had dressed for The Winter Gardens, in a warm, bulky coat.

Drivel and Rags had already made themselves at home in the back. Esmoylda got in behind the hula hoop, and as she and Stasia started pedalling the flippers, the cart moved forwards in a dramatically unpredictable fashion. They got used to it eventually, though.

'Where did he get all the materials to make it?' Stasia asked, as they started to get the hang of the pedalling, and picked up a bit of speed. 'Do you have the same problems here in The Sticks that we had at home, with plastic not being recycled?'

They were now bumping along the lane from The Gourds, leaving rainbow traces of paint from the leaking wheels as they passed The Lodge.

'I hate to tell you, but no,' replied Esmoylda, holding tight to the hula hoop as they turned by the old greenwold tree. 'We don't use plastic here. This is all made from driftplastic that's washed up along the banks of the waterways. It floats in on the tide from your world. Dad is fascinated by it.'

'Oh no,' said Stasia, as they flippered round onto the main road. 'I'm so embarrassed that our rubbish has clogged up your land!'

'Your land, too, now,' laughed Esmoylda, hauling the hoop back round to straighten up. 'You are officially a resident, remember?'

'Oh yes!' Stasia threw both arms up in air in celebration at that thought, as they passed the cobbled lane to the Middlepiddle bridge, surprising a passing splatdaw bird mid-flight. The resulting deposit woke Drivel up with a jolt, as it landed on his head.

Stasia laughed. 'That's supposed to be lucky, Drivel!'

'Not if it's you it lands on, it's not!'

They rumbled on past the turn-off to Bakington, which no longer had the tumbleweed on the horizon, which had been there a few months ago. The whole area had become lush and green; not just the Upper Bakington development to which Arton Mudd had diverted all the water, leaving the rest barren. It looked as if residents had returned to those cave houses that had been deserted when the water ran out, and it was all looking much more appealing.

'So, did you talk to your dad about living with your mum again?' Stasia asked Esmoylda, as they left Bakington behind.

'I started to,' said Esmoylda with a sigh, 'but I was competing with cogs, pulleys and dipsticks at the time, so I'll wait until the Transport Festival is over and try again.'

'This Transport Festival has been mentioned a few times recently, hasn't it? Is it a big event?'

'The biggest!' shouted Drivel, above the squeaking of the pedals. He was wearing sunglasses, his hair blowing in the breeze, and he was sitting on Rags so he could rest his elbow out of the window.

'Yes,' agreed Esmoylda. 'It is quite competitive, too. Everyone who enters a vehicle that they've designed and built thinks that theirs is the best. Especially the goblins and the gnomes. It can get nasty on occasions. There are a lot of other attractions there as well, though. It can be fun. And if we can't find out anything about Imperia at The Winter Gardens, we may need to go to the show and talk to her work colleagues at their stall. Good job we've got transport, because we may have a lot of travelling to…'

'AAAh!!!'

Esmoylda was interrupted by a shriek from Stasia, as her flipper pedal sheared into two pieces, throwing her foot forward and squashing her toe on the bottle chassis. Esmoylda stopped pedalling, and they coasted to the side of the road. They climbed out and stood scratching their heads, trying to work out what to do about the pedal. They were close to turning off into The Winter Gardens, and they could probably walk the rest of the way, but it wouldn't have been fair to abandon Clive's cart.

'Could we pull it to FG's house?' Stasia suggested.

'What?' exclaimed Drivel, who was lazy at the best of times, but especially now that he didn't have the Helpful Elf title to live up to.

'Maybe,' Esmoylda agreed, 'although it will get harder when we reach the snow.'

There was always snow on the ground in The Winter Gardens. As soon as you turned off the main road, it was just there.

'Rags!' cried Stasia. 'She might be able to help!'

Encouraged by treats that Stasia always kept in her bag, Rags jumped out and joined them at the front of the vehicle.

Realising what Stasia was planning, Esmoylda unravelled a couple of tree roots that her shawl was knitted from, tied them to the front of the cart, and then around Rags' chest, to form a harness. Stasia took some more treats from the bag.

'Look, Rags, your favourite. Come and get them.'

Rags' nose went into overdrive. Sniffing the treats, she moved forward to get to them, and the cart just about moved with her. It was heavy, though, and as soon as Rags had eaten her treats, she stopped moving and just looked around for more.

'I'll push from the back,' said Esmoylda. 'You walk in front of Rags, so that she pulls it.'

'Could you push, too, Drivel?' asked Stasia.

Drivel's face was a picture. He had been enjoying the thought that he might get to sit in the driver's seat and steer the cart. He definitely did not like the idea of pushing. Then he thought of a cunning plan. He pulled off one of the pieces of hosepipe from the body and picked off some of the stuff that looked suspiciously like chewing gum, sticking it on the end. Signalling to Stasia to throw him one of the treats, he stuck it to the chewing gum stuff. After attaching the hosepipe to the windscreen, using the irrigation tube, he climbed out onto the front of the cart, and onto Rags' back. Making himself comfortable, he waggled the pipe to get her attention, and she started moving forward, to get to the treat in front of her. And as she moved forward to get it, of course it moved forward ahead of her, and so she kept moving. And so did the cart.

'There,' said Drivel, to Stasia. 'Now you can push, too.'

'You cheeky…'

'Cheeky, maybe, but clever, don't you think?'

A smug elf is a happy elf, generally.

Chapter Seven

After the Party

They rolled up in front of Faerie Godmother's grand mansion, feeling hugely embarrassed. Especially as Drivel insisted on calling out cowboy phrases and singing *Rawhide,* as if he were driving a wagon. Esmoylda had sent a seed to FG, so she would be expecting them, and sure enough, she was there to greet them, floating gracefully on her front steps, not trying hard enough not to laugh.

'You made it then, flowers,' she said, giggling like a schoolgirl. 'Go on, treat yourselves to a little smile.'

Esmoylda and Stasia were dripping with sweat, despite the freezing temperature in the snow. Exhausted, dishevelled, and humiliated, they tried to comply with a smile, but it was painfully forced.

'Nip it round the back, flower,' FG said to a uniformed gnome at the foot of the steps, showing obvious disapproval. He dutifully snapped his fingers for three similarly dressed gnomes to come forward and move the cart away from the front entrance. Esmoylda untied Rags from the cart, Stasia helped Drivel into her bag, and they all climbed the steps and entered the awesome home of the Faerie Godmother. Esmoylda had to duck, of course.

The hallway was a labyrinth of corridors heading this way and that, and the busy, colourful pattern of the tiled floor added more confusion to the layout. There were multiple archways across each corridor, with twinkling lights suspended from them in loops. Signs on the walls declared such uplifting phrases as:

Make yourself at home
Do my laundry

And:

Life is better
When you are wearing substantial faerie bloomers

FG led the way, floating just above the ground. Esmoylda and Stasia whispered to each other, agreeing that FG was quite different from when they had last seen her, at the funeral. They liked her being bright and cheerful like this. Following her along one corridor, they turned left into another, and through the door at the end.

'Ta dah!' she sang, as she showed them into a sitting room with a twirl, then started laughing. 'I'm pleased to present to you the newly refurbished sitting room, of which I am extremely proud. And quite relieved, to be honest. You should have seen it a couple of days ago, after the party. What a state! I'm going to have to work overtime to pay the decorator, though. You didn't come, Drivel. Didn't you get your invitation?'

'I did, but I had to work, FG.' Drivel laboured the word "work".

While Stasia rolled her eyes, Esmoylda changed the subject quickly by commenting on the sitting room. After the overwhelming hallway, this was an oasis of calm. Big squashy sofas and armchairs, a roaring fire in a huge stone fireplace, and the most stunning view from an enormous bay window, overlooking a snow-covered landscape that was dotted with cottages and outbuildings. The oversized coffee table in the centre of the room sat on a rug of gently blended shades of lilac and blue, matching the luxurious fabric of the curtains and sofas. On occasional tables and sideboards were ornaments, awards, medals, photos in frames, piles of invitations and cards, and silver bowls of shimmering things. The clocks on the walls were feats of mechanical genius, with hands moving this way and that, and providing information about time, weather, politics, and anything else you might care to mention. Floating around the ceiling were probably hundreds of birthday cards, all with shining **300**s on them. They cast a sparkling glow over the whole room.

'This is so lovely, FG,' said Esmoylda, looking all around. It was a world away from her windmill home in Drainlands. 'I can't believe this was all decorated in a couple of days! Did you enjoy your party?'

'Ooh, yes thanks, flower. I can still handle a good night's partying, as long as I've had my tablets and I make sure I sit down from time to time. The karaoke was a bit exhausting, though. Great fun, but exhausting. Now, sit yourselves down, and tell me how I can help you.'

Feeling a bit big for the furniture, Esmoylda made herself comfortable on the floor, Rags curled herself up by the fire, and Stasia and Drivel sat on a sofa. FG floated onto her favourite fireside chair, put her dainty feet up on a furry footstool, and waited for them to speak.

'Do you know Imperia Jobsworth, who works for the Elf Service?' asked Esmoylda.

Drivel muttered something unrepeatable about Imperia.

'I know about the Elf Service, of course,' said FG, 'but that name doesn't ring a bell.'

'Her mother gave us this photo,' said Stasia, getting up and taking it to her. 'She's gone missing.'

'She asked us to investigate the matter!' Drivel piped up, pompously.

FG looked at him over the top of her glasses and smiled. 'Vanity, thy name is Drivel,' she misquoted. 'Of course,' she added to Stasia, 'your mother has taken on the Detective Agency, hasn't she? Clive told me. I'm sorry I haven't been able to help yet. I've been working my little socks off, getting ready for my party. But I do intend to get involved. You can rely on that.'

'That's great, thanks. Mum will be relieved.'

'But are you sure it won't be too much for you?' Esmoylda asked, in her usual caring role. She was looking up at all the birthday cards that were proclaiming FG's 300 years.

'Listen, sunshine, I'm not tucked up in bed at ten o'clock every night with a mug of cocoa, you know. I might be stuck here on my little lonesome, but you'd hardly expect me to sit here doing my knitting, would you?!'

'Apparently not,' Stasia laughed.

Esmoylda was mortified. 'I'm so sorry, I didn't mean to offend…'

FG burst out laughing. 'Takes more than that to offend me, flower.'

Relieved that she had only been teasing, Esmoylda got up to look at the photo with her.

'Imperia's mother is beside herself with worry. So we went with her to Imperia's apartment, and found your address, and the date of your party, with a photograph of you. Weirdly, there was some stage make-up as well, which didn't seem like something Imperia would use. I did wonder if your party was fancy dress? And if she was a guest?'

'No, she wasn't on the guest list. Not unless she came with someone else, but I don't recognise her. And no, it wasn't a fancy dress party, though it was very fancy. And we were all dressed. But that's it. There is something a bit familiar about her face, though. I just can't think why.'

Esmoylda showed her another photo. 'We are also looking for this goblin. His name is Arton Mudd, a gangster who's escaped from the Law Keepers. It's a separate case, but his henchmen turned up outside Imperia's apartment when we were there, so maybe there's a link. Or perhaps it's just a coincidence.'

'Ah, now… I have met him. Charming gentleman. He was at the party. Oh dear, sounds like my mental gangster radar wasn't working that night, doesn't it?'

Well, that wasn't something the detectives had expected. Arton Mudd was here, at the party. FG then went on to tell them that he had arrived with some friends, saying that they had been invited by Grig, a gnome from one of the Toasty Toadstool Cottages, who had said he was sure that she wouldn't mind. Grig couldn't remember having said this, but then he didn't tend to remember anything very much, so everyone accepted the story. Grig and his wife Gerky spent most of the party talking to Arton and his friends, and seemed to be having a lovely time, apparently.

'They were dancing and laughing,' said FG. 'Such a shame the evening ended the way it did, for them.'

'What happened?' Esmoylda asked.

'Well, apparently, one of Mr Mudd's friends came back from… somewhere… and had a message from… someone… that there had been a break-in at Gerky and Grig's cottage. He was very caring… apparently… and offered to take them home, to check that everything was alright. I thought that was kind… at the time…'

'Kind. Not a word I would have used for him... ever!' said Stasia.

'You know him well, then?' asked FG

'Oh yes,' said Stasia. 'I'll explain more another time. Did he take them home?'

'He took Gerky. Well, his friend did. On the back of his motorbike. And Mr... and Mudd went with the other one. Would you believe it!'

'Yes,' they said together.

'What were they up to?' Stasia asked Esmoylda.

Esmoylda just shook her head thoughtfully. 'Did they bring Gerky back, or pick Grig up?' she asked FG.

'One of the friends dropped Gerky back at the party, then left. We never saw any of them again after that. Gerky did tell me that Mudd had told her that she shouldn't have to miss out on the party, and should go and enjoy herself, and he would stay and clear up the mess for her. Although she said there wasn't any sign of the break-in, as far as she could see. But she thought he was so nice that she did as he said, and left him there to sort things out. I did speak to her the next day, and she said that in all honesty, there was more mess when they got home later than there had been before, so she thought he wasn't particularly good at cleaning up. As I'm telling you this, I'm starting to realise it's not sounding good, is it!'

'No, it's not,' said Esmoylda, thoughtfully. 'None of it adds up.'

'Gerky and Grig aren't far from here, are they?' asked Stasia. 'Could we walk there?'

'You mean you don't want to push your cart there?' FG had such a cheeky, girlish grin.

'Perhaps not,' said Stasia.

Chapter Eight

The Scene of the Crime

To say that Arton Mudd wasn't particularly good at clearing up was probably the understatement of year, judging by the state of Gerky and Grig's home a couple of days after the event. You could be forgiven for thinking that FG's party had been held there. As Gerky showed Stasia into the little sitting room, she remembered the last time she had been there, when she had desperately needed the loo. Gerky had been so kind, and given her a blanket, as she wasn't properly dressed for the climate.

Thanks to Drivel. She had been so grateful to Gerky that night.

As even Stasia had to duck quite low to enter Toasty Toadstool Cottage, Esmoylda had to stay outside with Rags. Drivel was keen to go inside, though, and "put his detective skills to good use".

The cottage was dark inside, because of the small windows, but normally very cosy. Today, it felt claustrophobic, though, with so many things out of place, and so much stuff lying around the floor. Stasia picked her way across the room carefully, to get to the sofa. Drivel took a different approach, and hurdled over the lot, onto the windowsill. While Gerky sat in an armchair facing Stasia, Grig was pacing around the room, occasionally tripping over things. He seemed agitated.

'He's been like this ever since the party, lovey,' said Gerky. 'I'm quite worried about him. He's got it into his head that there's more to this break-in than we thought. You see, nothing seems to have been taken. It's a very strange do. I can't make head nor tail of it, and it's really bothering the old man. He's been pinning notes around the dining room, and right across the ceiling. Then he's pinned string between the notes. He says he's trying to make connections between them. And he's not sleeping. His little brain is working overtime.'

'I lie on the dining table,' muttered Grig, 'and look at the whole picture. If I can see all of it at the same time, I might understand. Might know what's going on. Why did they come here? Who was it? Why? Who?'

'Don't get yourself worked up again, duck. Stasia and Esmoylda have come to help,' said Gerky.

Drivel cleared his throat.

'And Drivel,' added Gerky.

'Esmoylda is outside, Gerky. Maybe Grig would like to go and talk to her? She is probably the most sympathetic and calming influence you could ever hope to meet.'

Gerky agreed that anything was worth a try, and fetched Grig's coat. She led him outside, and his face lit up when he saw Rags, and after Gerky quickly explained the situation to Esmoylda, the three of them went for a potter about in the snow.

Back in the sitting room, Gerky told Stasia all about the events of the night of the party. This *extremely charming* Mr Mudd had spent the whole evening with her and Grig. Then one of his *lovely friends* came back from escorting some of the frailer guests to their taxis, and said he had just overheard a conversation about a spate of thefts in the area, and that one of them was at this very cottage.

'Quicker than greased lightning, Mr Mudd had me on the back of one of his friends' motorcycles, and he got on the other, and we were off. Grig stayed at the party. Mr Mudd said that would be best. Quite exciting, really, if I hadn't been worried about the break-in.'

'I hate to tell you, Gerky, but the man is a compulsive liar,' said Stasia, gently.

'How do you make that out?! That's daft talk.'

'I think you'll find…' Stasia stopped, realising Gerky wasn't ready to believe her yet. 'Sorry, Gerky, go on.'

'If you must know,' replied Gerky, 'he was a real gentleman. Helped me down from the pillion, and asked me for the door key, so that he could go in first and check that it was safe.'

'The door was still locked?'

'Yes… Oh… Yes, it was. They must have got in through a window.'

'And left through the window as well…'

'Anyway,' continued Gerky, 'he went in first. He was gone for a while, so he checked around thoroughly. After a bit, I followed him in, and I couldn't see anything had obviously been moved or taken, but he didn't want me to be upset by it, so he ushered me back out again, and said his very kind biker friend would take me back to the party and he would clear up.'

'And did he?' asked Stasia.

'Well, somehow, it was a lot worse when we got home than it was when I had seen it earlier. And poor old Grig has been really anxious ever since. So muggins here has been trying to go through everything carefully, before putting it away to see if anything is missing. And my corns are giving me jip, and I can't get around too quickly these days, especially since being on the motorcycle, and it's all a bit…'

She took off her glasses and wiped her eyes.

'Do you really think he's a wrong 'un?'

'I know he is, I'm afraid, Gerky. He's on the run from the Law Keepers. Amongst other things, he held my mum and Esmoylda hostage, to get me to pay money that someone else owed him. It's a long story, but you can't trust him, or his mates.'

Gerky's jaw fell open. 'Oh, lovey. I had no idea. No idea. Oh dear.'

'Don't worry, Gerky. We'll find out what he's been up to. Would you like me to help you clear up?'

'Oh, would you, lovey? Thank you. Grig might feel calmer if everything is back where it should be. But what was he doing?

Making all this mess? He must have done it after I was taken back to the party, I suppose.'

Stasia started picking things up from the floor. 'Have you noticed if anything is missing?'

'That's the strangest thing, my duck. No.'

They worked together, tidying up and putting things away. Drivel "helped". As the sitting room became clearer, Stasia commented on the beautiful curtains and cushions.

'All my own work,' said Gerky. 'I've been sewing since I was a little gnomelet. I make all FG's gowns, and do any repairs for her, too. Sometimes I get to do some for the Faerie Queen, as well,' she added proudly.

'That is impressive,' said Stasia, looking around for a sewing machine. 'Where do you work?'

'I've got a workroom through the back. Would you like to see?'

Gerky led the way through to the back of the cottage and into a darkened room off the kitchen. She went to the window and opened up the shutters.

'I haven't been in here since the party. Too busy trying to sort through things and minding my Griggy, poor old sausage. I can't think that Mudd would have…'

As the light flooded the room and Gerky turned around, she stopped talking and just stared. Even in her beloved workroom, things had been pulled out of cupboards and drawers, and off hanging rails. Her scissors and threads were all over the floor, and her sewing machine was on its side. She sat down and she sobbed. Stasia tried to think what her mum would do now, so she went into the kitchen and made Gerky a cup of tea. As thick and puce as she could manage. After Gerky had had a few sips, she looked suddenly concerned. She scoured the room with searchlight eyes, as if something might be hiding from her.

'Oh no! Oh no! That doesn't make any sense!' she cried. 'Faerie Godmother's new gown. It's gone!'

'Really? Are you absolutely sure?'

'Yes, it was on that rail. I had just finished it. It has layers and layers of tulle and laceworm threading, you can't miss it. It's definitely gone!'

'That's just weird,' said Drivel, joining them to see what was going on. 'Mudd in FG's dress? It would never fit him.'

'There must be something else going on here,' said Stasia.

Chapter Nine

The FG Machine

Stasia, Esmoylda, Drivel and Rags made their way slowly back across the snow to FG's. They were deep in thought, trying to work out just what Arton Mudd was up to. By the time they reached their destination, they were no closer to finding the answer. Or working out where Imperia Jobsworth fitted into it all. If, indeed, she did. They joined FG in her sitting room.

'Well, I think it's all about selling your clothes to the highest bidder,' declared Drivel.

'Really?' said Stasia. 'Are they worth that much? Who would buy them? '

'I have many admirers, you know,' said FG, mock-offended.

'What I can't work out, though, is why he didn't just take a dress from here!' said Drivel.

'He would never have been able to take anything from here,' said FG. 'I have the best gnome security around. They would have noticed anyone going where they shouldn't.'

'But how would he know that Gerky would have one?'

'Ah,' said Esmoylda, 'I think I might have the answer to that one. While I was walking with Grig, he told me about meeting Mudd and his men at the party, and how chatty they were, and so interested in him and Gerky. Grig couldn't remember much of the conversation, but he knew that he had told them how proud he was of his wife, baker of great riddleberry crumble, and dressmaker to the beautiful Faerie Godmother.'

'Oh, you're just saying that.' FG pretended to blush. 'Right, ok then, flowers, we are starting to get somewhere. Arton Mudd came here to get one of my dresses. He couldn't get one here, so he sweet-talked Gerky and Grig, and made up a false reason to get into their cottage. Agree so far?'

They all nodded.

'So,' she continued, 'and here's the biggy... WHY?!'

They all shook their heads and shrugged their shoulders.

'Nope, I haven't got a twinkly inkling, either.'

✡

The next morning, Esmoylda picked Stasia up in an altogether different mode of transport. This time, they were travelling in style, in FG's pride and joy, just as they had when they came home the day before.

Realising they were getting no closer to finding out what had gone on there, they had decided to get back to looking for Imperia. And without any clues as to why she had FG's photo and address, or if she had any link with what Arton Mudd was up to, the only lead they had left was to find her work colleagues. They knew they were going to be at the Transport Festival that day, so that was where they needed to go next.

On hearing this, FG had asked if they would take her entry for the competition on her behalf, as she felt she should stay and look after Gerky and Grig. Also if they would mind leaving their cart behind, and take her stunning self-propelled carriage instead.

They thought about it for one hundredth of a second, then said: 'Oh, alright then.'

They couldn't believe their luck, having an elegant and stylish carriage to travel home in. They had cheekily said that she was welcome to use the cart until they were able to return the carriage to her. Mysteriously, she said that would not be necessary.

So off they went to Expatland, in search of clues as to the whereabouts of Imperia Jobsworth. Dorissa and Snooch were having no luck tracking down the mob. Apparently, they had gone back to Koolton to try to find them, but nobody knew where they were. Sarah had sent them back to the lodge, to sort out their paperwork (or to get them out of the way), and agreed that all they could do for now was try and track down Imperia, and maybe she would be able to tell them more.

Gliding along in the extraordinary carriage bearing the number plate **FG I**, the intrepid trio felt extremely important. It was so relaxing to travel in, too, as it drove itself. They did ask Sarah if she wanted to come too, but she was having far too much fun stripping wallpaper. Rags stayed at home this time, as they were all concerned for the beautiful upholstery in the back of FG I. Stasia had made Rags squash into the footwell on the way back from FG's.

It wasn't a long journey to Expatland, along meandering country lanes, and they found the event easily. Actually, they didn't find it at all - the carriage did. After floating down the tree-lined driveway, making them feel like royalty arriving at the venue, it then even took them to the allotted space in the competition ring, marked with FG's name and competitor number, then parked itself up facing the judging area, and shut itself down. The shiny faerie sculpture that posed on the bonnet of the carriage folded her wings, gracefully sat down, and crossed her legs.

'Well, if this beauty doesn't win the overall show prize, I'll eat my hat.'

As Esmoylda, Stasia and Drivel were dismounting from the carriage, the voice came from behind them. They all turned to see a well-built troll with a familiar, kind look around the eyes.

'Monty!' Esmoylda threw her arms in the air, ran up to the stranger, and hugged him.

Stasia and Drivel looked at each other. They had never seen their friend behave like this before.

'Stasia, Drivel... this is Monty!'

Stasia smiled politely, none the wiser, and Drivel said bluntly, 'Who?'

'My brother!'

'Oh! So nice to meet you,' said Stasia, stepping forward to shake his hand.

'Is Mum here?' asked Esmoylda, excitedly.

'No, sorry, she was too busy. Are you alright? I've just seen Dad, and he said you're playing detectives?'

'Playing? *Playing?*' Drivel was leaping up and down with rage.

Monty turned to Stasia and winked.

'Funny,' Esmoylda groaned. 'We are actually looking for a missing person. But we're also looking for a rather nasty goblin gangster, who has escaped from the Law Keepers. And we don't know, but we think there might even be some link between the two. Or not.'

'You don't know much yet, then, do you?' he said, teasing. 'And who does this beautiful beast belong to?' Monty gazed admiringly at FG's carriage.

Esmoylda and Stasia briefly outlined the story of the cart, and yesterday's visit to FG. Monty laughed heartily at the idea that they had even attempted to travel anywhere in Clive's mock-up plastic pedal cart. But he was immensely impressed that they had arrived today in *The FG Machine*, as it was listed in the programme.

'Well, good luck to you all. It sounds like you've got a lot on your plate. I've got an entry in the competition as well, so I'd better go and make sure it's looking its best. And I'll catch up with Dad, too – we're in the same category. See you soon.' Monty kissed Esmoylda on the head and disappeared through the growing crowd.

With tears in her eyes, Esmoylda watched her brother walk away.

'You need to talk to your dad,' said Stasia. 'Tell him how you feel about the family living separately.'

'I know,' Esmoylda sniffed. 'But he's always so busy.'

'After the show, maybe.'

'After we've found Imperia Jobsworth, and captured Arton Mudd!' said Drivel. 'So come on!'

The first step was to find the stall that the Elf Service were running, and talk to anyone who had been working with Imperia recently. The troll they had met at the apartment block was just setting up the promotion boards on the stall, with a faerie who was dressed in a similar fashion. Esmoylda asked if they had any information about Imperia that would help, and when they last saw her. It seemed that the faerie had noticed a change in Imperia's behaviour in the few days before she disappeared. She had been secretive, and defensive, she said, although she was never the easiest to work with, so it was quite hard to tell the difference. But as it turned out, after she stopped turning up for work, the manager noticed that some files had gone missing. They contained personal information about the children that came to the department for their Helpful Elves (Drivel cringed at the mention of the term), and about their families.

'That's a surprise, don't you think, Drivel?' Stasia asked, as they weaved their way through the stalls being erected. 'I didn't like her, but I thought she was devoted to the job, the way she quoted the rule book at me.'

'I didn't like her 'cos she shut me in a box,' was Drivel's only contribution.

'It sheds some light on what she was doing before she left her job, but not why, or where she is now,' said Esmoylda. 'We're not much further on, really, are we?'

'Is she? Is she really? *Faerie Godmother?* That's a surprise!'

Stasia and Esmoylda looked at each as they overheard FG's name being mentioned by a complete stranger walking past. They were Expats, from Stasia's old homeland.

'Well, that's what I heard,' said the other. *'Running the self-help seminar in Blickly Manor. First session today.'*

'A self-help seminar?' Stasia said. 'What's that when it's at home?'

'I'm not really sure,' said Esmoylda, 'and I don't remember FG mentioning it, but Blickly Manor is only just over there – just a little further along from this field – and she said she couldn't come to the show today, didn't she? Unless she couldn't bring the carriage because she was doing that instead. Shall we go and find her? And find out what a self-help thingummybob is?'

'Why not?' said Stasia. 'Drivel could certainly use some help with himself.'

Chapter Ten

Gaining Entry

The archway marking the entrance to Blickly Manor was festooned with fliers advertising the self-help seminar. And, sure enough, dominating each one was a photograph of FG. Esmoylda took one of the fliers from the wall, and looked at it closely. She read out the details of lectures to be given by Faerie

Godmother, on *Self-Discovery and Well Being* and *How to be Present in Your Own Head.*

'What?' said Drivel.

'Exactly,' said Esmoylda. 'I can't imagine FG even saying those phrases, never mind lecturing on them, can you?!'

Stasia was laughing too much to answer straight away. 'Especially not the second one!'

'I think we need to go and see this for ourselves,' said Drivel, marching off towards the front doors of the manor. 'You said there's one starting soon, so let's go in!'

'Hang on, Drivel!' Esmoylda was waving the poster, trying to get his attention.

'What's wrong?' asked Stasia. 'Don't you want to go in? I do. I won't believe this until I see it!'

'No, it's not that, it's just that I don't think Drivel has realised how much it costs.'

They watched as Drivel approached the main doors, and spoke to the uniformed goblin on duty. Drivel exclaimed loudly and the official gestured for Drivel to go away. They cringed as they saw that Drivel was not going to leave quietly, and was obviously upsetting the nice goblin and driving him to use language unbecoming of a doorman at a self-help seminar. As soon as they had stopped laughing, they collected Drivel, dragging him away.

Drivel was not impressed by the way he'd been treated, and it took quite a while for the girls to calm him down. He said he had only asked politely to be allowed in without paying, because he and the Faerie Godmother were "like this" – and crossed his fingers. Apparently, that means something completely different in the goblin culture, and the doorman was offended.

'You gave us a good laugh, anyway,' said Stasia, then ducked as he threw his hat at her.

'Did you catch sight of FG in there?' Esmoylda asked him. 'It stills seems hard to believe that she's giving these lectures. How did she get there? We had her carriage. And she could have brought it herself, anyway.'

'I'm glad she didn't, though,' said Stasia. 'It was great riding in it. Did he tell you where to get the tickets, Drivel? Before he threw you out, that is?'

'Funny. No, he wasn't being that helpful. Actually, he was not helpful at all after I said we were close to FG. I think he made that up about being offended. They're too thick-skinned for that.'

'It's true that goblins aren't known for their sensitivity,' agreed Esmoylda.

'So you think he didn't want to let you in because you know FG? Not because you didn't want to pay?' Stasia asked doubtfully.

'You always think I don't know what I'm talking about. I have got a brain, you know.'

'But are you *present in your own head?* 'asked Stasia with a smirk. Then she felt a bit guilty for sounding so sarcastic. 'Actually, I have heard Mum talking about "being present". It's supposed to be good for you, to concentrate on the here and now, instead of worrying about the future. Something like that, anyway! Perhaps there is something in these seminars, after all.'

'Maybe we should pay to go in, and see if there is anything strange going on,' Esmoylda suggested. 'We're here now, and have no idea where to find Miss Jobsworth, or Mudd. If we could get to see FG, and tell her what we learned from the Elf Service administrators, she could advise on what we should do next.'

'It's a lot of money, though, isn't it?' Stasia was still getting the hang of the new currency. '150 chubbies sounds like a lot.'

'It is. Why don't we just steal the badges?' suggested Drivel.

'What badges?' asked Stasia.

'The badges that everyone was wearing going into the building. If they had a badge on, he just let them in.'

'Well, perhaps we could *borrow* some badges, just to get us in to see FG? If we don't actually attend the lecture then it wouldn't really be stealing, would it?'

'I like your thinking, Esmoylda,' agreed Stasia. 'Where do we get them from, Drivel?'

'Well, they all seemed to be coming round the corner of the building, from the back.'

'Perhaps there's a ticket office there. Let's go and see.'

They set off with the most innocent expressions on their faces that they could manage. The place was buzzing with expats: people who had emigrated to The Sticks from the world Stasia and her mum had come from, but had all settled together in the same area, living as much as possible in the same way as they had before. They were living in a comfortable bubble of people who shared their own background, rather than living with the locals.

As Stasia listened in on some of the conversations, she could hear the people referring to the locals as 'they', and complaining about 'them'. It didn't sound very friendly, or respectful. In fact, it sounded as though the expats thought they were better than them. Fair enough if they were all like Arton Mudd, but what about Esmoylda? And the Faerie Godmother?

Turning the corner, Drivel groaned. And the others could see why. The doorman had now moved round to the ticket office. He was just taking over from the goblin taking the money and giving out the badges. It looked like it might be harder than they thought to get hold of some, until Stasia had an idea.

'Esmoylda, if you hang back a minute, I'll go and speak to them. I look like most of the others in the queue, so they won't notice me so much. But Drivel, come with me.'

Stasia stepped forward, but signalled to Drivel to wait a little way behind. Esmoylda watched from the cover of a nearby tree, as Stasia approached the goblin at the desk just inside a doorway, turning and pointing towards Drivel. The goblin got up with an air of urgency, pushed his chair backwards, and ran towards Drivel, who turned and scampered away, disappearing into the crowd. By the time the breathless goblin had returned to the desk, with no sign of Drivel, and plonked himself back in his chair, Stasia had returned to Esmoylda's hiding place.

'Come on,' she said, leading Esmoylda away.

'Where's Drivel?' asked Esmoylda, concerned.

They rounded the corner to the front of the building, where Drivel was waiting for them by the main doors. Stasia handed them each a visitor's badge.

'How did you do it?' Esmoylda was impressed.

'She used me as bait!' Drivel was not impressed.

'I told him I wanted to buy a ticket, but I was really scared as I was being followed by a suspicious-looking elf,' said Stasia, laughing. 'As soon as he saw who it was, he went off like a rocket.

Then it was easy to grab the badges and go. You did really well to get away, Drivel.'

'No thanks to you. You didn't give me much warning. I would have stood further back if I'd known what you were going to do!'

'It wouldn't have looked so believable if you'd known. You're a terrible actor.'

'True,' said Esmoylda. 'But well done, Drivel. So now we can go in, and hopefully get to talk to FG. We can tell her that her carriage is delivered safely, too.'

'Well, *it* delivered *us* safely,' said Stasia.

They went in through the main doors, and flashed their badges at the new doorman. He looked twice at Esmoylda and Drivel, but nodded them through when he saw the proof that they had paid. Or not, in this case.

Inside the manor house, there were people milling around in the foyer, and most looked strangely familiar to Stasia. Almost like she was back in her old life again, amongst old friends and neighbours. And yet she didn't feel at home with them. She could hear them complaining about things that were a normal part of living in The Sticks.

Trolls move too slowly when you are in a hurry in the supermarket.

Goblins are grumpy (well that's true)

Some faeries just think they are "it".

Stasia wanted to suggest to them that they go out into The Sticks and meet and mix with the locals, and get to know them. But she didn't want to bring attention to herself when she was not there legally, and she wanted to find FG.

'I'll send her a seed,' said Esmoylda, who was getting some strange looks. Some very well-dressed women were looking down their noses at her (although they had to tilt their heads back to do so), and she was feeling quite uncomfortable. This made Stasia cross, and ashamed to be of the same species.

'Good idea,' Stasia agreed loudly, showing her clear solidarity with her best friend, a troll.

'They're going in,' said Drivel. 'What shall we do?'

Esmoylda launched the seed, expecting it to fly down the corridor from the foyer, which was emptying fast. Instead, though, it nipped straight out of the doors and across the fields, climbing high into the sky.

'No!' cried Esmoylda, 'It must have been a faulty one. It's gone the wrong way!'

'We'll just have to go into the lecture after all, then,' Stasia suggested, seeing the doors to the hall were about to close. 'We'll listen to her lecture and come out being more *present in our heads!* Then we can talk to her afterwards.'

They nipped in through the lecture hall doors just as they were closing.

Chapter Eleven

The Seminar

They took seats in the back row of the lecture hall, so as not to be conspicuous. Esmoylda was already attracting a lot of attention, and they didn't want to make things awkward for FG. Drivel perched on the back of Stasia's seat. Esmoylda was looking around over the tops of heads, for any sign of an incoming sycamore seed, but nothing so far. Stasia was quite excited about seeing FG again so soon, and listening to what she had to say. She just couldn't imagine what it was all about.

There was a ripple of anticipation going around the room as

some music started up and a door to the side of the stage opened. Stasia craned her neck to see. Drivel stood up on the back of the chair and toppled down the back. He let out such a screech of panic as he got wedged between the seat and the back wall. Stasia and Esmoylda got up and moved their chairs forward to get him out, making a terrible scraping sound on the floor. The rest of the audience were turning round and telling them to be quiet, and complaining loudly that they knew *they* would be trouble when they first set eyes on *them.*

During all of this kerfuffle, the music stopped abruptly. The door next to the stage had closed again, and nobody had appeared. Then there was even more mumbling and grumbling, and pointing of fingers towards the back row, even though the trio were sitting quietly waiting now. Esmoylda was mouthing "sorry" to as many people she could catch the eye of. Drivel glared back at them. Stasia stared forwards, as if she were completely unaware of what had just happened.

Eventually, the room quietened down again, and the music restarted. Expectation grew in the audience, but the door remained firmly closed. The little four-piece band in the corner began to sound less confident, and gradually tailed off as, one by one, each musician stopped playing, until only the tin whistle was left. The pixie playing it was in a little world of his own, until the big boggart on the bassoon dug him hard in the ribs. Silence fell in the room and Stasia held her breath, although she didn't know why. A goblin standing by the door to backstage opened it a little, whispered in harsh tones through it, then closed it again. He cuffed the ear of the hob on the oboe, and the band started up once more.

The audience sat up straight in their seats and waited. The door opened again, and the skirts of a glorious gown appeared through the opening, followed by the dignified form of Faerie Godmother herself. She gave a harsh look to the goblin by the door, and pushed roughly past the musicians as she headed for the stage, causing the troll on the triangle to miss a beat. FG climbed the few steps clumsily, tripping on the top one, and just managed to stop herself from falling flat on her face. She muttered something that visibly shocked a couple of buttoned-up ladies in the front row.

'Is she alright?' Stasia whispered to Esmoylda.

'It doesn't seem like it, does it?' Esmoylda was puzzled. 'She is usually so happy and friendly. Perhaps she's nervous?'

'Is that why she's not floating, do you think?' asked Drivel.

Esmoylda and Stasia turned to look at him. Of course. Faerie Godmother hadn't floated as she normally would. Now settled in position on the stage, she started to address the audience. She read from a wodge of notes, with a dull, monotone delivery, asking rhetorical questions about how people felt about themselves, and how they could improve their self-esteem, etc., etc., etc.

'Not very inspiring, is it!' whispered Stasia.

'Perhaps it will get better as she relaxes,' sighed Esmoylda, hopefully.

'This is rubbish,' said Drivel.

'She was rude to the band when she came out, too, wasn't she?' said Stasia. 'That's not like her.'

'I keep wondering why she didn't tell us that she was doing this,' said Esmoylda. 'Perhaps we could have helped her prepare, or something.'

Through an open window on the other side of the hall, a seed appeared, and started to circle above the heads of the audience, distracting Faerie Godmother from her speech. She shouted out that everyone should have cancelled the delivery of all sycamore seeds during the lecture. She then went on for several minutes, about how rude it was to interrupt a performance with such selfishness, and could she please be allowed to continue uninterrupted. She began to try to sell the audience a residential course called *Feeling Good in Your Own Skin,* and insisted that it was of vital importance for their well-being in their new lives here in The Sticks, and imperative that they take up this opportunity, or they would desperately regret it later. At this point, the goblin by the backstage door, along with several others, moved swiftly around the audience with forms for them to sign up to the residential course, handing out pens so they could fill them in there and then.

'So, let me get this right,' said Stasia. 'The audience have paid to come to the lecture, which has mainly turned out to be an advertisement for a residential course, which costs even more money.'

'FG must have cash flow problems,' said Drivel.

'I think there's a lot more to this,' said Esmoylda, holding up the seed that had dropped into her lap a few moments before. 'This is from FG!'

'What?!!!' Stasia thought she must have misheard. 'From FG? Even though she's on stage right now?'

'Yes.'

'That's clever,' said Drivel.

'That doesn't make sense,' said Stasia.

'No,' said Esmoylda. 'It doesn't. And, she has no idea what I meant when I said we were here, and hoping to meet up with her afterwards.'

'Sorry???' Stasia was completely bemused.

'Also, she says that she has discovered that a spare pair of spectacles and a tiara are missing from her home.'

'Did she say what the tiara looked like?' asked Stasia, staring at the stage.

'Yes,' said Esmoylda. 'Just like that one.'

All three of them stared at the figure on the stage. She looked like FG. She sounded like FG, although a rather terser tone than usual. But she was rude and mercenary, she was not floating, and actually, on closer inspection, her wings looked completely different. Most importantly of all, she was wearing a stolen tiara.

Whoever it was on stage, it was not FG.

Chapter Twelve

Who is She?

They were trapped. Having realised they were witnesses to some sort of dodgy goings on, they now wanted to leave as quickly as possible. But there were expats seated on each side of them, and the goblins were closing in. There was no way that they would be signing up to the residential course, but the goblins were intimidating each member of the audience, by leaning over them until they signed, as they made their way along the rows. And goblin breath has never been known for its sweetness. Suddenly, Drivel jumped down off the back of the seat onto Stasia's lap and shouted, 'I'm going to be sick!'

Everyone along the row, from Stasia to the aisle, leapt up out of their seats and cleared the way. Stasia tried to keep a straight face as she lifted Drivel above her head and she and Esmoylda squeezed past them all, saying sorry and thank you. Drivel clamped his hand over his mouth and somehow managed to make his snouty little face go green. It must be an elf trick. They ran out of the hall, through the foyer, out into the grounds, and collapsed in a heap, sighing with relief.

'Well done, Drivel,' said Esmoylda.

'Genius,' said Stasia.

'Always a tone of surprise,' said Drivel.

'Ok,' said Stasia, 'now what do we do?'

'Nothing else for it,' said Esmoylda. 'We're going to have to tackle that imposter.'

'We've already got two cases on the go,' said Drivel. 'How much more are we expected to do?'

'You can go home if you like,' said Stasia, crossly. 'I'm sure Mum can find you some decorating jobs to do.'

'No, it's ok. I was only joking.'

'Where is she most likely to leave backstage?' Esmoylda wondered. 'I don't suppose she'll come outside, so there must be a back corridor inside the manor, maybe near the kitchens? We need to catch her, and find out who she is, and what she's playing at, as we're the ones on the spot, and we've witnessed it all.'

'You always have to do the *right thing*,' muttered Drivel.

'Unlike you,' said Stasia. 'Shall we go and find another way in, before we miss the chance to catch her?'

They hurried around the outside of the manor, and eventually found a door leading straight into the kitchen. The hobs getting refreshments ready for the guests were too busy to pay them any attention. They carried on through into a corridor and looked left and right, deciding in which direction they were most likely to catch the imposter. And just as they were discussing it, she came through a door along the corridor and headed away from them, tripping on the hem of her gown and cursing as she stumbled in her high heels towards the private rooms.

'Hey, you!' shouted Drivel, before Stasia could shut him up.

The false FG turned her head to see who had shouted, then turned back and ran. Not far, though, as she caught her toe in the hem of the gown, and went head over heels along the corridor, in a highly undignified manner. It was extremely fortunate that she was wearing substantial faerie bloomers that day. When she eventually stopped somersaulting, she just leant back against the wall and sobbed. Her wig was crooked, her glasses awry, and the tiara was hanging from one ear. Her thick make-up was smudged and tear-marked, revealing a different complexion beneath it. On catching up with her, the three of them stood and stared.

Esmoylda started to feel sorry for her. 'I'm sorry, but we know that you're *not* Faerie Godmother. We need to know who you are, and why you're impersonating her. She is a friend of ours.'

Before the imposter could even draw breath to answer, if in fact she was going to, Stasia and Drivel spoke together:

'Imperia Jobsworth!'

Esmoylda turned to them with eyes wide open. 'Are you sure?'

'Well?' Stasia said to the imposter.

The fake FG struggled to her feet, swamped by the voluminous gown. As she stood up as straight as she could, she pulled off the wig, to reveal the thick, dark locks of Imperia Jobsworth. She took off the glasses and produced her own signature oversized pink pair (from a pocket in her bloomers) and put those on instead. And there she was. Imperia Jobsworth. Not, it has to be said, looking her best.

'How did you know?' she asked, with a tremor in her voice.

'We've met,' said Stasia. 'You gave me *him.*' She pointed to Drivel.

'Did I? Well, I hope he was *Helpful.*'

'Not really, but I've got used to him.'

'And I'm a detective now!' Drivel squeaked. 'You're nicked!'

'Drivel, we don't have the powers to 'nick' people!' intervened Esmoylda. 'But we have been looking for you, Miss Jobsworth. Your mother is extremely worried about you. And now we find you are involved in something... dodgy... to say the least. We'd like you to explain it to us, please.'

At this point, Imperia Jobsworth broke down in uncontrollable sobs, which was probably the last thing that Stasia and Drivel would have expected from her. But she also seemed scared, and wanted to get away from the manor, so they gathered around her, and with Esmoylda behind her, blocking her from anyone's view, they bundled her through the kitchens and out of the building, without being seen.

'Have you got any of your own clothes with you?' Esmoylda asked Imperia, when they had reached the safety of a clump of trees.

'No. He wouldn't let me keep my own clothes here. He said I wouldn't be needing them, and he would bring them to me when I did.'

'Who?' asked Stasia.

Imperia broke down again, and it was some time before she could answer. 'Arton Mudd.'

They were all stunned into silence for a moment.

Drivel was the first to speak. 'This just gets weirder.'

And so the story came out. It seems that Arton Mudd had charmed Imperia, making her believe that he genuinely liked her. They had met "by chance" one day, in the park where she usually went at lunchtimes. After a few more meetings, he asked her if she was able to get some information for him. He had spun her a story about a family that had come to live in The Sticks, and rented a property from him, then absconded without paying the rent.

'Sounds familiar,' said Stasia.

He wanted to find out more about them, so that he could get the money he was entitled to, and he had guessed that there would be a file about them in Imperia's office. She had felt sorry for him. And he was so nice to her. She gave him a recording that had been made, of the child's visit to the office when he came for his Helpful Elf.

'A recording?!' said Stasia. 'You mean, you secretly record the interviews?'

'I do, yes!' said Imperia Jobsworth, defensively. 'What's wrong with that?!'

'I think we had better go back to that one later,' said Esmoylda. 'Carry on.'

Apparently when children visited the office, they could be quite chatty, and would tell the administrators quite a lot about their families. Stasia couldn't imagine telling Miss Jobsworth anything, but perhaps not everyone felt the same. And when Mudd had this recording in his possession, there was enough information on it for him to blackmail the family into paying their rent. And more. Imperia was mortified, but to make matters worse, he now used what she had done for him to blackmail her into giving him information on a regular basis. She was like a fly caught in a web.

'But how did you come to be here, impersonating Faerie Godmother?'

'He made me do it,' she sobbed. 'I think he only pretended to like me, not just because I work for the Elf office, but also because I look like Faerie Godmother… except for the complexion… and the hair. And I can't float.'

They all turned to stare at her, scrutinising her face.

'Oh yes!' said Drivel.

'I'd never noticed that!' agreed Stasia.

'So that's why FG thought there was something familiar about your photo,' said Esmoylda. 'She could see a likeness to herself, without realising that's what it was.'

Chapter Thirteen

The Truth is Out

Imperia Jobsworth continued with the whole sorry tale. It was Arton Mudd who had set up these self-help seminars, given by the famous "Faerie Godmother", knowing that they would appeal to the expat families. And at the first lecture, his goblin employees would move around the audience with registration forms for the very expensive residential course, which, of course, was not worth the money. But as the goblins stood over the audience members, asking them to sign, they also whispered a little of the information Mudd knew about them, blackmailing them into signing up.

'I wondered why so many of them were signing,' said Esmoylda, 'when – no offence –the lecture really wasn't... well... it was good, but... it wasn't...'

'It was rubbish,' said Drivel.

'I know,' snapped Imperia, 'but it wasn't my fault. He just wanted Faerie Godmother there to bring in the crowds. Everyone loves a faerie godmother, apparently.'

'Of course,' said Stasia.

'He stole the dress and tiara and glasses. Gave me stage make-up to make myself look more like her. He must have been planning this all along. I feel such a fool.'

'If it makes you feel any better,' said Esmoylda, 'you're not the only one to be taken in by his charm. He went to Faerie Godmother's party and tricked Gerky into letting him into her cottage, to steal that gown that she had made for FG.'

'Even after that, she found it hard to believe he would do such a thing,' added Stasia.

'How do you know all this?' asked Imperia. 'How did you find out what he was planning? How did you know where to find me?'

'We had no idea you were here. We came to the Transport Show to speak to your colleagues, then we heard that FG was giving a lecture. We had only just left her, so we were curious, and decided to check it out,' Stasia explained.

'And we had no idea what Arton Mudd was up to. We were looking for you and for him, for different reasons, and it was a complete surprise just then, when you said you were mixed up with him,' said Esmoylda.

'We found out about the theft after going through your things in your apartment, and discovering the details about Faerie Godmother's party, with a photo of her and the make-up. So that's where we started,' said Drivel, proudly.

At this, the old Imperia Jobsworth made a reappearance. **'You went to my apartment?!!! You went through my things?!!! How dare you!!!'**

'Now, wait a minute,' started Stasia.

'You can't speak to me like that anymore. I'm a detective, I am!' declared Drivel.

Esmoylda raised her hand for calm. 'We went there with your mother, at her request,' she said. 'We were looking for clues as to your whereabouts.'

Stasia and Drivel looked at each other, impressed once again with Esmoylda's professional manner.

'Your mother was so worried about your disappearance that she had contacted the Law Keepers. They didn't take her concern seriously, so she contacted us. The only place we could start looking was your apartment. We spoke to your neighbours, and...'

'You spoke to my neighbours?!!!' Imperia interrupted.

'Imperia Jobsworth! Will you get off your high horse!!' No more Miss Nice Troll. Esmoylda was taking control. 'We spoke to your neighbours. And it was a good job we did, or we wouldn't be here now. That's how we found out that your office had a promotional stall at the Transport Festival, and we came here to speak to them.'

'Oh, I forgot about the stall. I was supposed to be there. So they know I'm "missing" now, do they?'

'Yes. And, by the way,' added Stasia, 'your mum is feeding your kattles for you.'

'Oh yes! Good. Ok.'

'A "thank you" would be nice,' muttered Drivel.

'Why? You didn't feed them!' Imperia Jobsworth was still finding it hard to be nice.

'Well,' interrupted Esmoylda, 'we still need to find Arton Mudd. I've just sent a seed to Sarah, to find out if Dorissa and Snooch have had any luck tracking down Riz and Raz. I'm guessing that Mudd isn't here, is he?'

'No. He likes to stay in the shadows. But he won't be far away, as he also likes to keep a close eye on his investments. The Transport Festival is near here, isn't it?'

'Yes,' said Stasia. 'It's in the field next to these grounds.'

'He's probably there, then. Close enough to be in control, and mingling with crowds to stay out of sight. Not to mention he loves his vehicles. More than anything else,' Imperia added with a touch of bitterness.

'We'll go over and nick him, then,' said Drivel, simplistically.

Imperia Jobsworth turned to look at Drivel in bewilderment. 'Have you got any idea what you are dealing with?'

'Ignore him,' said Stasia. 'But yes, we know exactly what we're dealing with.'

A sycamore seed dropped into Esmoylda's lap. She opened it and read it quickly. 'It's from Sarah. It seems we still don't know where Riz and Raz are, although I think we can probably guess they will be somewhere near Mudd. She says the Law Keepers are on the way to pick you up, Imperia. You'll have to go with them and tell them everything, but Sarah has also contacted your mum, so she'll meet you there.'

'Oh no. She'll be in a total state.'

'At least you'll be safe,' said Stasia.

'But you'll have to face the consequence of your actions,' said Drivel, gleefully.

'I think she knows that, Drivel,' said Esmoylda.

After a few minutes, the Law Keepers arrived. They looked surprise to see Imperia in an astoundingly glamorous gown, that didn't fit very well, melting make-up, and grasping a wig and a tiara. Not your usual attire for getting arrested. They took her away to the offices, to be charged for her part in the fraudulent plan, and for passing on private details of clients. Ignoring Drivel's inappropriate sniggering, Esmoylda suggested that they go back to the festival, which they could hear was getting well underway now. The Law Keepers had called to them as they led Imperia away, not to go and look for Mudd on their own. They impressed on them that it was much too dangerous for them to go after him. When they had agreed to the agency tracking him down, they had meant for them to report anything back that they found out. Not to go after him themselves. So, had they made themselves clear?

'Yes,' said Esmoylda, Stasia and Drivel.

Now, back at the festival, they seemed to have forgotten that they were not supposed to be tracking Mudd down. They started searching in earnest. The event was heaving with visitors now, many of them dressed in costume. There were expats dressed as goblins and faeries, and goblins and faeries dressed as Elton John and Lady Gaga. They explored between the vehicle exhibit arenas, and further afield, where the tents and caravans were set up by the competitors that had come from some miles away. Some awnings were there with no vehicle attached, presumably for vehicles that would be brought back from the arena later. After looking around, they began to explore the stalls, selling anything from food and drink to mini collectible model vehicles from previous years' winners: carriages that could fly; carts that turned cartwheels; bicycles that could recite their times tables.

There were so many people and creatures milling around the stalls, it was difficult for any of them to see anything. Especially Drivel. But then Esmoylda stopped in her tracks and pointed. Unfortunately, Arton Mudd looked up from the model of the tap-dancing amphibious tank that he was studying just at that same moment, and saw a familiar troll pointing straight at him. He dropped the model, much to the annoyance of the stall holder, who started shouting after him. As did the exhibitor whose bicycle went flying as Arton knocked it over in his haste to get away. Then an argument started near the cake stall.

Esmoylda and Stasia started running in the direction of the cakes. It seemed likely that the uproar that was growing there was because of Mudd. When they reached the stall, they found a troll and two faeries arguing, but no sign of Mudd. Apparently, he had told the faeries that the troll had taken a cake, and then disappeared into the crowd, leaving them arguing. An obvious distraction technique. And it had worked. He was nowhere to be seen.

'Where's Drivel?' asked Esmoylda.

'Oh no!' exclaimed Stasia. 'I don't know!'

Chapter Fourteen

The Car Show

Just as that feeling of overwhelming panic was about to set in, which comes when someone is lost and you just can't see them anywhere, a group of protesting gnomes jostled past. They were heading for the centre of the crowd, to get maximum attention. They passed the Female Faerie Institute stall – where *Jerusa Jam* was being sung in close harmony – and the open barns holding workshops on spigot-making and *How to wire your widget,* then on into the main arena, where the vehicles were lined up, ready to be judged. The placards they held aloft declared that events like this draw too many visitors, who carve up the countryside and endanger local wildlife. Not in so many words, though. More like: ***Go home, you vehicular nutters!*** And ***Leave our froghogs in peace!***

As the protesters marched past Esmoylda and Stasia, a little voice shouted from in amongst them. 'He's over there! Come on, follow us!''

And there he was, Stasia's very own Helpful Elf, actually helping, sitting bold as brass on the shoulders of one of the marching gnomes. From his vantage point, Drivel had spotted Mudd heading for the arena, so Esmoylda and Stasia followed on. As they entered the arena, Stasia grabbed Drivel from behind and pulled him off, before he got himself in trouble, or got lost again.

'Well done, Drivel, but now stay put!' She deposited him in her bag.

'OK. But can you see him?' Drivel asked urgently. 'Don't lose him!'

'I can see him,' said Esmoylda. 'He's mixing in with the competitors, as if he's got a vehicle in the show. I doubt he has, though.'

'I shouldn't think so,' agreed Stasia. 'He would need to be able to keep going over to Blickly, to check on the seminar. He probably just thinks we wouldn't look for him here.'

'How shall we go about this? Shall I find Dad to help us?' asked Esmoylda.

'Great idea,' said Stasia. 'You go and find him, and I'll keep an eye on Mudd from here.'

But, just as Esmoylda slipped off into the crowd, the announcement came that the judging was about to start. Stasia tried to call Esmoylda back, as she could see Clive on the other side of the arena, by his vehicle. The protesters had been removed from the arena and were hanging around the edge, mumbling loudly. The judges moved in and around the ring, looking at the vehicles and making notes, discussing their thoughts and findings with each other. And all the time, Mudd was mixing in with the competitors, as if they were his best friends, although he was also looking around shiftily. He was a goblin on the run from the law, after all, and he knew he had been spotted once.

When the judges had finished their deliberations, a sprite flew in with a bell, ringing it for the crowd to be quiet as the announcements were made. Clive came second and was thrilled to receive his award. He looked so proud.

Stasia looked around, to see if Esmoylda had returned in time to see him win it. But she was nowhere to be seen, so she clapped as loud as she could, and whooped and called out his name on Esmoylda's behalf. Clive looked over and gave her the thumbs-up. Then the first prize was announced.

'… and the first prize goes to… Faerie Godmother! For her highly imaginative and unique gliding carriage. We believe she cannot be here today, so is there someone who can take the award on her behalf?'

Stasia wasn't sure what she should do. Where was Esmoylda? She tried to catch Clive's eye, but he was too busy showing his award to members of the crowd, and pointing out features on his automobile.

Drivel popped his head up. 'Go on, then! Go and get it! What are you waiting for?!'

'But I'm supposed to be watching Mudd! If I go up, he'll see me, and know that I 've recognised him, won't he?'

'Oh, yeah.'

During the time it took for Stasia to think all this, however, someone had already snatched the prize, and jumped into the carriage. Stasia screamed out, 'Stop that goblin!!! Stop him! It's Arton Mudd!!'

But it was too late. The gates had been opened, and the carriage was starting to move. He was not only going to get away again, but he was stealing FG's carriage as well. Stasia spotted Esmoylda heading back to the arena.

'He's there!' she shouted to her. 'He's in FG's carriage! He's getting away!'

Everyone was becoming aware of what was happening, but nobody was sure what to do, or whether they should get involved. Instead, they were turning to each other, and discussing what should be done about it, and by whom. Hopefully, not by them. But when Esmoylda saw what was happening, she rushed to the gates, and tried to close them again, before Mudd could drive through. Stasia was too far away to help. She started pushing through the crowd around the outside of the arena, heading towards the big gates, watching Esmoylda trying to close them on her own, in time. She got caught in a crush of onlookers, who were so determined to keep their places while they watched events unfolding that Stasia couldn't get past them. But Esmoylda wasn't alone. Monty had arrived, and was helping her by closing the other gate. Esmoylda had asked him to help when she couldn't find Clive, and now they were working as a team, like they had when they were young.

Mudd was not one for giving in easily, though. He let out a piercing whistle, and almost immediately his motorcycle henchmen roared in, parting the onlookers, and blocking the gates from shutting. They sat on their machines, like a guard of honour, as Mudd made his way through in the beautiful FG I. In a last-ditch attempt to stop him, Esmoylda leapt into the path of the carriage, shouting **'STOP!'** She held up her hand in defiance and stood her ground firmly as Mudd continued to advance.

He was not going to stop.

Even in front of a crowd of witnesses.

He couldn't put his foot on the accelerator, as it didn't have one, but he kept moving towards Esmoylda.

She was not going to get out of the way. She was so incensed by the fact that he was stealing FG's pride and joy, and sure that he would have to stop.

But he didn't.

There was a scream, and the carriage and the motorcycles were gone.

Chapter Fifteen

Brotherly Love

Stasia forced her way through the rubberneckers, pushing with all her might. By the time she reached the gates, Clive was there too. He was crouched on the ground, cradling his child, and shouting for help. At last, some of the crowd started to get involved, and somebody ran for the medical crew. Stasia tried to comfort Esmoylda as she stood and cried.

'I thought it was you,' Stasia said softly, looking down at Monty on the ground.

'He pushed me out of the way,' sobbed Esmoylda. 'He saved my life. And now he's...'

'... fine,' said Monty, from his dad's arms. 'I keep telling you, I'm absolutely fine. Well... maybe not absolutely. But I'm fine-ish.'

'It could have been a lot worse, though,' said Clive, sombrely. 'What did you both think you were doing? Why didn't you come and get me?'

'You were busy,' said Esmoylda, with a slight, uncharacteristic, edge to her voice. 'You are always busy.' She finished a message to FG, telling her what had happened, and sent it on its way.

The medical crew arrived just at that moment. They had been planning to put Monty on a stretcher, until they saw the size of him. Two little faeries were not going to be able to manage a troll of Monty's proportions.

'I'll take him,' said Clive, and scooped Monty up in his arms, carrying him effortlessly to the First Aid tent. 'You two get home and stay safe,' he called over his shoulder.

'What about me?!' shouted Drivel from Stasia's bag.

'You too, I suppose,' said Stasia, not in the mood for Drivel's grumps.

'Rude,' said Drivel.

Chapter Sixteen

In the Courtroom

Amidst the smells of old damp wallpaper, and fresh new paint, Stasia and Sarah were getting ready to go to court. Drivel was even wearing a tie, of sorts. It was a neon shoelace from Stasia's old trainer, but it worked. Stasia was quite excited, as she had never been to a courtroom before.

Sarah was much more cautious. She had not wanted to get caught up with running the agency in the first place, and was only doing it until FG could take over. Seeing Stasia involved in a situation like this was not the start to their new life in The Sticks that Sarah had been hoping for. It had been bad enough a few months ago, when they first arrived, but that was not out of choice. She regretted letting her daughter and Esmoylda follow up the Imperia Jobsworth case. But, in her defence, she had thought it was a simple missing person scenario. Dorissa and Snooch were supposed to be on the trail of Arton Mudd. But somehow Stasia and Esmoylda (and Drivel, of course) had accidentally managed to solve both cases at the same time.

It turned out that after Mudd had run Monty over and escaped from the festival, the carriage had taken him straight back to FG. It had a built-in homing instinct. And when FG had received Esmoylda's message, she knew that would happen, and had arranged for the Law Keepers to come and await his arrival. Apparently, when Riz and Raz realised where Mudd was heading, they peeled off in a different direction, and headed back home to their mums'.

And now they were all going to court, to witness Arton Mudd's prosecution. Somehow, the case against him for holding Sarah and Esmoylda hostage had resulted in just a fine, which he had asked to be added on to his regular payments of fines, from a whole list of other misdemeanours. So perhaps today was not going to be any different.

*

Stasia and Sarah took their places in the courtroom alongside Esmoylda, Clive, Monty, and a lady troll with Esmoylda's kind eyes. Without a shadow of a doubt, this was Esmoylda's mum. Esmoylda was sitting between her mum and her brother, linking arms with both, as if clinging on for dear life. Apart from the slight wince from Monty as Esmoylda squeezed his arm tightly, he seemed to have recovered from being run over by Mudd. In fact, when he had tried to describe the feeling of the carriage driving right over him, he said that it felt as if it had just floated across, and he wasn't seriously hurt at all. This was no thanks to Mudd, though, as his mum pointed out.

Dorissa and Snooch sat in the row in front of them all, fidgeting with excitement. At the front of the room, a goblin was sitting at a desk, ready to take the notes of the case. Another goblin stood by the door, ready to usher in the witnesses. In the first row were the legal representatives, both of whom were goblins. And the goblin for the defence was… Arton Mudd himself.

'He's conducting his own defence!' gasped Sarah.

'What does that mean?' asked Stasia.

'It means that he will be the one asking Imperia questions. She is the main witness against him in this blackmail trial. She made a deal with the courts, so she won't be prosecuted for her part in it.'

'What does that mean?'

'She isn't in trouble, because she is helping the authorities against Arton Mudd.'

'And who is that?' As the door at the front of the courtroom opened, the usher ordered everyone to stand up for Judge Peewit. Entering the room was an elderly goblin wearing elderly robes, stooping, and leaning heavily on a gnarled and twisted walking stick. Even with his thick, round spectacles, he seemed to be struggling to see where he was going. He bumped into the usher, then knocked over the glass of green gloop that had been placed on the rail around his bench. On his instruction, everyone sat down once more.

As Esmoylda and Stasia were too young to give evidence, and FG and Gerky had given their statements in writing, Imperia Jobsworth was the only witness for the prosecution to appear in court. She entered the room unsteadily, and stepped up to the witness box, clinging on to the front to keep herself upright. Her normally aggressive manner had vanished, and she looked a shadow of her former self. The prosecutor got up from his chair and approached her. After getting the formalities out of the way, checking her name and address and so on, he began the questioning.

'Miss Jobsworth, can you please tell the court, in your own words, how you came to meet Mr Mudd, and what happened after that.'

Imperia started to tell the story that she had told the young detectives when they'd helped her escape Blickly Manor. How Mudd had obviously been watching her for a while, and knew where she went at lunchtimes to be able to "bump into" her. (The prosecutor said that they could not prove that. It could have been coincidence.) She went on to tell the court that Mudd had charmed her and persuaded her to steal information (the prosecutor said that he might not have meant for her to do it), and that he then blackmailed her, too. (The prosecutor said that "blackmail" was quite a strong word to use. The judge agreed.)

'The prosecutor is supposed to be on Imperia's side!' whispered Sarah, loudly.

Dorissa turned round. 'What is he playing at?'

'Who's playing what?' asked Snooch.

'Silence in court!' called the judge.

The prosecutor said that was all, and the judge asked Arton Mudd if he had any questions for the witness. Mudd got up and walked towards Imperia. Everyone in the room held their breath. Imperia Jobsworth backed away from him, quaking.

'Imperia. My dear. Are you ok?' Mudd was using those slippery, silvery tones that Stasia had heard the first time she met him. 'I'm sure the good judge wouldn't mind if you sat down. Would you like a drink?'

Imperia Jobsworth looked puzzled. And then almost relieved.

'She's falling for it!' Sarah was incredulous. 'He's pretending to be nice, and she is falling for it all over again.'

Imperia accepted the drink, but remained standing, so that she could see over the witness box.

'Now, tell me my dear,' continued Mudd, 'you don't really think I was just using you to get information, do you? What on earth put that idea into your pretty little head?!'

'But… but…' Imperia was thrown by the charm. 'I thought you were pretending…'

'No, no, no, no. Of course not, *Impywimpy.* I *so* enjoyed your company, and the pleasant walks and picnics we had together…'

Even Snooch looked puzzled. It was awfully hard to picture.

'… and nobody was more surprised than I when you offered that information to help me to get back only what belonged to me. I thought it *must* be legal, or you wouldn't have done it! It was *terribly* nice of you.'

A sharp intake of breath could be heard around the courtroom.

'No… no… that wasn't how it was.' Imperia was beginning to realise too late what game Mudd was playing here. She was on the back foot now. 'I didn't offer… you asked…'

'Oh dear, there must have been some misunderstanding,' said Mudd, calmly.

The prosecutor nodded. The judge nodded.

'The seminars!' Imperia shrieked. 'You stole from Faerie Godmother and made me dress up!'

'Oh, didn't you look lovely,' oozed Mudd. 'That was *so* nice of you to wear that lovely frock for me. Where did you get it again?'

'You got it! *You* got it!

'I think perhaps you got an incey-wincey bit jealous when I went to FG's party, didn't you? And that I helped her lovely dressmaker when she had a break-in? Did you go back and get the dress later? Were you trying to impress me? I thought you were a little overdressed for the self-help conferences you were running. I did think they were such a good idea of yours, though. Trying to increase self-esteem in our new residents. So lovely of you. I think perhaps you went a bit far by using your job at the Elf Service to get information about them, though. I know you were only trying to help them. We all know that, don't we?'

The judge and prosecutor nodded.

'No more questions, Your Honour,' he finished.

'That's not how it was!' screamed Imperia Jobsworth, shaking, and sobbing, as she was dragged away from the courtroom.

'Do you have any witnesses you would like to call, Mr Mudd?' asked Judge Peewit.

'Yes, Your Honour. I would like to call two, but would it be alright with you if they came in together? It would mean you could get off early for lunch.'

'Oh, that's good of you, Mr Mudd. Thank you.' The judge nodded approvingly.

Clive held his head in his hands in despair.

'Call Garf and Nostrils,' said Mudd.

'Oh no,' said Stasia and Esmoylda, together.

'Are they…?' Sarah began.

'Mudd's trainee mobsters,' said Stasia. 'They will just do anything he tells them to.'

'So, Garf,' started Mudd, when the two weedy goblins (who Esmoylda had hoped never to see again) were squeezed into the witness stand together.

'Me… me… ask me…' interrupted Nostrils.

'So, Nostrils,' Mudd started again…

'Me… me… ask me…' interrupted Garf.

'Shut up!' shouted Mudd, losing his cool. The prosecutor and the judge were visibly shaken, and bent their heads, so as not to bring any attention to themselves.

'Gostrils!'

'Yes,' said Garf and Nostrils, accepting the new joint nickname without argument.

'Did you ever see me anywhere near Blickly Manor, at Miss Jobsworth's seminars?'

'No. Never.'

'Did you ever see me asking for money from anyone in Expatland?'

'No. Never.'

'They weren't there!' said Stasia to Sarah.

'I rest my case,' said Mudd.

'Well, I think that has cleared that up,' said Judge Peewit, standing to leave.

'Yes, I think that is satisfactory,' said the prosecutor, getting his sandwiches out of his briefcase.

There was uproar in the room from Sarah, Stasia, Dorissa and the troll family. Snooch was asleep.

'This is a whitewash!' shouted Dorissa.

'You can't believe this rubbish, Judge?!' shouted Sarah, much to her own surprise. 'He's a thief and a blackmailer!'

'Silence in court!' called the judge, bowing his head to hide his face as he moved towards the door. Mudd smirked.

'What about my son getting run over?' shouted Monty's mum.

'Oh yes,' said Mudd, turning to face the gallery. 'Sorry about that. Didn't see him.'

'And the theft of Faerie Godmother's carriage?' called Clive.

'What theft?' said Mudd. Then he added coolly… 'I was just returning it.'

Chapter Seventeen

The Unwelcome Visitor

So once again, Mudd got away with it. The court had ruled that he had no charges to answer, and he had walked out of the courtroom a free goblin. But it was not too long before he started causing trouble again. He was not one tiny little bit happy that Imperia Jobsworth had the audacity to give evidence against him. Arton Mudd was fiercely defensive of his intimidating reputation.

A reputation for being in charge.

A reputation for being feared and respected.

A reputation for not letting *anyone* get away with *anything*.

Imperia Jobsworth was in her apartment, cleaning, tidying, and generally clearing out any evidence of Arton Mudd, so she could reclaim her life as her own, when there was a knock at the door. It struck fear into her. She knew that knock. That knock told her she had no choice but to open the door, or things would get even worse. She was going to have to do a lot of grovelling. Tentatively, she unlocked the door and pulled it open.

'Hello, my dear,' said Arton Mudd.

'Hello,' Imperia replied, in the smallest of voices.

'Aren't you going to invite me in? I've missed you.'

'Oh... yes... come in.'

He moved slowly past her, while she stood to one side. As she closed the door behind him, the neighbours watched and whispered. Arton Mudd made himself comfortable on the sofa, while Imperia Jobsworth perched awkwardly on the edge of a chair.

'You don't look relaxed, *Impywimpy*. Why would that be?'

'No, Arton, I'm fine. Honestly.'

'I'm not convinced, my dear. You are very tense. Why is that? Could it possibly be because you feel you let me down, and you feel guilty about it? Is that it?'

'Yes, that's it.'

'Oh, don't be silly. It's not your fault that the Law Keepers persuaded you to get yourself off the hook by blaming me for everything, is it?'

'No.'

'No?'

'I mean yes.'

'Yes. Yes. I suppose it is your fault really, isn't it! *You* impersonated Faerie Godmother. *You* stole personal files from your place of work, in order to extort money from unsuspecting expats. Then *you* told the courts it was *me*. Yes, I think we can definitely say that it was all your fault. Can't we!'

'Yes.'

'Yes. Did you think you could blacken my name and upstanding reputation, while you casually went back to your boring little life, and just carried on as normal?'

'No.'

'No! That is not how it is going to be. Luckily, I have friends in high places, and they could see how unfairly you were treating me. How you were spreading vicious lies, out of jealousy and spite. That it was really you that had committed the crimes. If you hadn't tricked them into making a deal to keep yourself out of jail, that is exactly where you would be right now. Isn't it?!'

'Yes.'

'So, I am going to see to it that it is *your* reputation that is ruined. Your life will never be the same again. You will never be able to stop looking over your shoulder, just in case I am there. Do you understand?'

Arton Mudd didn't need an answer. Imperia Jobsworth was nodding, and shaking with fear, tears streaming down her face. He got up and walked over to the door without saying another word. But as he opened the door to walk out, he half turned his large head, and, for the benefit of the neighbours who were gathered around on the landing, waiting for more gossip, called, 'Goodbye, my dear. Hope you are feeling better soon.'

'Morning, ladies,' he said to the neighbours, collectively, as he closed the front door. 'Looking lovely today.'

They twittered like birds. Flattery always went down well with them.

He started to descend the staircase and met Muriel a few steps down. She was huffing and puffing her way up the stairs, with several bags of shopping.

'Can I help you with those?' he asked her, and took all the bags in one swift movement, before she could answer. 'Where are you going?'

'Oh, thank you, the third apartment on the left,' she said, breathlessly. 'But aren't you…?'

'Arton Mudd. At your service,' he replied with lashings of smarm. 'And with those beautiful looks, you must be Imperia's mother, Muriel.' Actually, he had seen a photo in Imperia's apartment a little while ago, and knew exactly who she was.

'Oh,' said Muriel, caught off-guard. She had been ready to hate him after all she had heard from her daughter. 'Yes, I am, actually. Have you been to see her?'

'Yes, I just called in to see if she was alright, after all that has gone on. Poor thing is quite exhausted by it all. I don't think she had meant to do anything wrong. I think she just got herself in a bit of a pickle. Don't you, Muriel?' He put the bags down by the front door.

'Oh, yes… perhaps that was it, then… do you think? But she said…'

'Oh, I know she thought it was down to me. Perhaps it was my fault. Perhaps I should have realised sooner that she wasn't quite herself. But I hadn't known her long, so…'

'Oh… dear… do you think… perhaps it was my fault? Should I have noticed that she was behaving differently from normal? The things she told me about you, then? They weren't quite… accurate?

'Well, it's not for me to say, Muriel. I'm just worried about her.'

'Oh dear. Well, I'm going to stay with her for a few days. I'll keep an eye on her.'

'Oh, are you?' That wasn't quite in Mudd's plan. 'That's nice. Mind you, I wouldn't take too much notice of her ramblings, Muriel. She is really not too well. I think she may have had a bit of a breakdown. She probably needs a bit of space.'

'I'll feed her up and give her lots of Mummy hugs,' said Muriel, putting her key in the door.

'If you must,' Mudd muttered, turning away. He wasn't happy about Imperia having anyone on her side. He would have to do something about that.

☆

From then on, Mudd made sure that he always knew where Imperia Jobsworth was, every minute of every day. When she went to the shops, or to work, or the library, he would be standing on the corner, or in a shop doorway, or behind a shrubbery, watching her. And he made sure that she saw him. If she hadn't noticed him, he would cough loudly, or sometimes even call her name. But if Muriel were with her, he would make sure he bobbed out of sight when she turned round, if Imperia tried to point him out. He was clever. It was only ever Imperia who saw him. And Muriel became quite concerned about her daughter. She thought that either she was imagining it, or that she was obsessed with getting Arton Mudd into trouble.

And so the next time Muriel "bumped into" him, when she was shopping on her own, she was quite ready to believe what he told her. He was all smiles and sympathy, asking how Imperia was. She told him what had been happening (from Imperia's point of view) and he was *mortified* that anyone might think that he had actually been following her. Why on earth would he do something as hideous as that?! He was so fond of her. What could he do to convince Muriel that he was not that kind of goblin?

'I'll talk to Imperia,' said Muriel, reassuringly. 'I'm highly optimistic that I can get her through this sticky patch.'

'Oh, I do hope so, Muriel. She is so fortunate to have you as a mother. If only I had had a mother like you…' Mudd wiped away a "tear". 'Really, though, are you sure it is the right thing to do, to prop her up, and wrap her in cotton wool? Do you think it might be better to make her stand on her own two feet, so that she gets stronger again? Only a thought, of course, Muriel. You know best.'

'Well, I…'

'I'll leave it with you, Muriel. I know you will do the right thing by her.'

'Well, I…' she said again, but Mudd was gone.

Chapter Eighteen

Mothers and Daughters

'I've just been chatting to your gentleman friend, dear,' said Muriel as she struggled in through the front door with the shopping bags. She took them straight into the kitchen, followed by Lorry and Hardel, and an extremely animated daughter. After depositing the bags on the table, Muriel turned round to put the kettle on, to be faced with a full-on tirade of indignation.

'My *gentleman* friend?! *My* gentleman friend?! My gentleman *friend*?!!'

'Shall I make us some tea?' Muriel thought a nice cuppa would defuse the situation.

'Don't you understand *anything* I've been telling you?' blustered Imperia, while Muriel made the tea. 'He is *ruining* my life! He is *stalking* me! He *lies* through his horrible *teeth*! He is making my life a *misery*! He follows me *everywhere*! He is *grinding me down*! He *hates* me! **He threatens me!** Are you listening??'

'Yes, dear. Drink your tea while it's hot.'

He is a nasty, scary creature!'

'Well, I think… perhaps… he hides a lot of emotion beneath that placid exterior…'

'What??!!!'

'Drink your tea, dear.'

'I'm not in the mood for being humoured, Mother…'

'I just think you need to buck up a bit, Imperia. Mr Mudd said perhaps it would be better if I don't wrap you in cotton wool, and make you stand on your own two feet…'

'"Mr Mudd" said that, did he?! And since when were *you* so pally with Mr Mudd that you listen to *him* rather than to your own daughter?!!!!!!'

'Don't shoot me, I'm just the errand girl,' said Muriel. 'He just seemed to want the best for you…'

'Best for me????!!!!!'

'Stop repeating everything I say, Imperia. Really, what is the matter with you, dear? I don't know what to say for the best, anymore.'

'Say nothing, then, Mother. If you don't believe anything I say, I don't know what you're doing here!'

'Well, since you have brought the subject up, perhaps it is time I went home. Mr Mudd said…'

'Well, if Mr Mudd said it, it must be right! Go! Just go!! Get out!!!'

'I'm going. You have always been prone to touches of malice and spite, Imperia dear. I'll just leave you to have a little think about that. I'll get my things together, and I'll be off. Do you want any more tea?'

In no time at all, Muriel was packed up and packed off home. Unbeknown to her, her exit from the apartment block was witnessed by a figure in the shadows, his collar turned up against the wind. Arton Mudd allowed himself a smug smile as he watched Imperia Jobsworth's only ally heading off down the road with her suitcase. He was enjoying the thought that he had driven a wedge between Imperia and her mother, and that she was probably up in her apartment on her knees, emotionally. He began to laugh. But then he thought he would just go and check on his handiwork before he started to celebrate. He crossed the road and opened the main door to the apartment building. As he entered the lobby, he could hear voices on the landing above, so he stayed out of sight and listened.

Imperia had opened the front door and had held it open until her mother was ready, and she was still holding it open after her mother had gone. She didn't really know what she was doing. She was beside herself with anxiety about how Arton Mudd was destroying everything in her life, bit by bit. And that even her own mother believed him rather than her. While she was standing in the doorway, her work colleague had arrived home. She paused on the way to her apartment to speak to Imperia.

'Hello, Imperia. You didn't come in today! How are you?' she seemed concerned, but Imperia didn't trust anyone anymore.

'Why do you care?' she answered, brusquely.

'I'm sorry. Has something else happened? I thought you were feeling better, with your mother staying with you.'

'I've got a couple of days off. Not that it's any of your business. And my mother isn't staying anymore. She's gone.'

'That's a shame. By the way, I think you should know that Arton Mudd came into the office today. I thought he might have come looking for you, but he seemed to know that you wouldn't be there. He asked to see the manager, so Angustura invited him into her office, and he spent quite a long time with her, drinking tea and talking. And then they were laughing. I thought it seemed odd. He seemed in incredibly good spirits when he came out, and was complimenting everyone in the office as he left. I thought he was a bit creepy, myself.'

'What was he doing there?? He's going to get me sacked, isn't he! He is a creep! He's a slug! He's a lying, blackmailing, smooth-talking snake!! Why can't people see that? My own mother, even!!!'

During this uncontrolled outburst, which Mudd was enjoying enormously from a hidden corner of the lobby, the Elf Service employees had been joined by Duster and Facepack, who had come out to enjoy the sideshow.

'Is that Arton you're ranting about? Well, he was awfully nice to me,' said Facepack, patting her curls. 'Very charming, I thought.'

'Always a lovely smile and a compliment,' agreed Duster. 'Always makes you feel good.'

The little troll from the office thought she would nip into her apartment before Imperia exploded again.

'You don't know what you are talking about! He's a stalker! A manipulator. He will make anyone believe anything he wants them to!!'

'He wears great suits,' said Facepack.

'Nice shoes,' said Duster.

And they turned around and went back into their respective apartments. As both doors closed, Imperia Jobsworth collapsed in her doorway, racked with sobs, crying out the question: *'Why won't anyone believe me?!'*

Arton Mudd smiled a wicked smile and left the building. His work here was done for now, but he still had another trick up his sleeve.

☆

When Imperia ventured out of the apartment the next morning, Mudd was waiting. He watched her as she left the building, and followed her along to the shops. When she spotted him, because he made sure that she did, she tried to turn back and run for home, but he blocked her way.

'What is your hurry, Imperia, dear?' he said loudly, to show passers-by that he knew her. 'You look terrible. Come with me, and I'll buy you a koffee.'

And with that, he took her arm so firmly that she had no choice but to go with him. He smiled at everyone that they passed, all the time gripping her arm so tightly that it hurt. And she didn't dare complain. Perhaps she even allowed herself a little hope that he did still like her, and wanted to start seeing her again. But any hope of that was dashed once they had sat down at a little table in the corner of Kelvin's Koffee Korner, and the hob waitress had taken the order.

'Thought we could have a chat,' Mudd began, 'about you bad-mouthing me to everyone. That's not nice, now, is it, my pretty?'

Imperia could only shake her head.

'You tried it with your mother, but that didn't work, did it? I put a stop to that. Just as I have with your manager at work. I don't know how you managed to keep your job there after what you did. You must have done some serious grovelling, but they won't keep you on now. Not now that I've told them you can't be trusted, because you have already offered to steal for me again. That you're not sorry for anything you've done, whatever you might tell them. And that you deliberately broke down in court so that I would not be convicted. That it was all an act on your part. Charming, your manager. I think she was quite taken with me. We had a pleasant chat over tea.'

Mudd casually leant back in his chair and looked at his watch. As the hob brought the koffee to the table, she noticed Imperia brimming with tears, and shaking as she took the mug.

'She's not been well,' Mudd reassured the waitress. 'I thought it would be a change for her to come out for a while. And this is such a marvellous establishment. Where better to put a smile back on her face?'

There was no smile on Imperia's face, until Mudd kicked her ankle under the table.

'That's right,' said Imperia. 'Thank you.'

The hob was surprised, as she knew Imperia as a regular customer, who normally complained about everything, from the thickness of the koffee to the colour of the mug. She was always rude, and usually tried to get at least one of the waiting staff sacked every time she came in.

'She *must* be ill,' she muttered to the other waitress as she returned to the kitchen.

Imperia forced down the koffee, wanting to get home as soon as possible. Mudd didn't drink his. He just sat and stared at her, unblinking, making her feel as uncomfortable as possible. He didn't even make conversation, leaving her to stew on what he'd said. And every now and then, he made a point of looking at his watch. Eventually, he said, 'What time is it?'

She looked at the clock. 'Half past twelve?' she faltered, wondering if this was a trick question.

'That should do it then,' he said mysteriously. And he left.

Imperia Jobsworth sat at the table alone, relieved that he had gone, worried about what he was up to now, and feeling awkward and embarrassed in front of the koffee house staff. Needing to regain a little dignity in her own mind, she wiped her eyes and straightened her glasses, rose from the table, and, as she walked out, she said: 'Call that koffee? It tasted like something from the Stinking Swamp!'

That made her feel a bit more like her old self. She went in one or two shops to get the food shopping she needed, checking carefully each time that Mudd wasn't there. Then she returned to the apartment and closed the door behind her with a sigh of relief.

Taking the shopping into the kitchen, she called out to Lorry and Hardel. She would usually have heard them purring long before they appeared, but the apartment was eerily silent. She called their names again as she got the kattlefeed out of the shopping bag. Still nothing.

That churning feeling that comes with the realisation that something awful might have happened, but you don't want to believe it – that was what Imperia was feeling right at that moment. She ran from room to room, virtually screaming Lorry and Hardel's names. Searching under beds, on top of wardrobes, in kitchen cupboards, out on the windowsills. Not a sign. But the door had been locked! How could anyone have taken them?!

She sent a seed message to the only other key-holder for her apartment, to ask if she knew anything about it. The reply came almost straight away. Muriel said:

"How could you think I would take Lorry and Hardel?! Don't be silly, dear. Anyway, I don't have the key at the moment. Mr Mudd asked if he could borrow it to pop in and sort out your plumbing."

Imperia Jobsworth went cold. What more could he do to her? Not only had he alienated her from her family, and friends, if she had had any, but he had got her the sack from her job, and now stolen her precious kattles. She was angry. This was the final straw. She would make sure he was punished for this.

But then she realised.

She was his alibi.

Chapter Nineteen

Lorry and Hardel are Missing

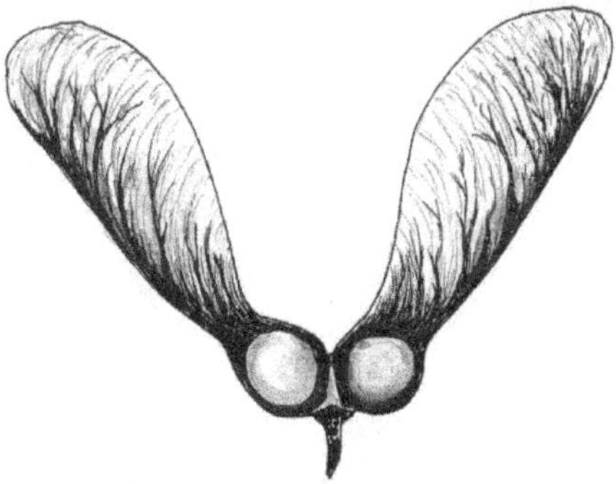

Even as Imperia sent the message to the Law Keepers, she knew it probably wasn't going to be any use. She told them that her kattles were missing, the door was locked, and that Arton Mudd was the only one to have a key apart from her. When the answer came back, it wasn't any great surprise - although the P.S. gave her slight hope.

Dear Miss Jobsworth,
Hope you are feeling a bit better than when we last saw you in the courtroom. You were a bit of a mess, weren't you! Emotionally -

stable - wise?

We always take complaints seriously. However, we have contacted Mr Mudd, and he denies everything. He says he has given the key back, deciding not to use it after all, as he didn't trust his own plumbing abilities. Extremely sensible, we thought. Leave it to the professionals. And as for the timing of the alleged incident, he said he was with you. So it could not have been him. Unless it was you and him? But if it was you, you would not be making this complaint. Would you?

Hope this clears up the matter,

Law Keepers' Office, Expatland.

P.S. On the matter of the disappearance of Lorry and Hardel (nice names), we feel that this is another fine mess you have got into, but we happen to like kattles at the office, so we will send someone out to look for them.

Imperia Jobsworth felt about as low as she could be. She had lost just about everything, including her pride, so she might as well completely demean herself and ask for help. Even if it had to be from the Faerie Detective Agency.

✡

Sarah was at the top of a set of stepladders, painting the sitting room ceiling, when a sycamore seed flew in through the open window, hit her in the eye, then dropped into her paint pot.

'Oh no! Stasia! Help!' she called as she carefully descended the steps with one eye closed, holding the pot of paint and the brush.

Stasia ran in, with Esmoylda close behind, both wearing masks, and covered in dust from sanding the staircase. While Sarah bathed her eye, Stasia and Esmoylda retrieved the seed from the paint, and washed it under the tap in the kitchen. It was pretty soggy and, as they tried to open it, bits got stuck together. They could read enough to know that it was from Dorissa, and that she was asking them to come to The Lodge. But as to why, it was too severely damaged to read.

'Oh well,' said Sarah, checking that her eye could open, 'we had better get over to The Lodge, then. Well, I had, anyway. I did say I would be there for them. You can stay here and carry on if you like?'

'No, we'll come too. The sanding will still be here when we get back… unfortunately,' said Stasia. 'What do you think?' she added, turning to her best friend, and laughing at the state of her.

'Er, yes, I think it would be good to get out of here for a bit and catch up with Dorissa and Snooch. Not that I mind sanding. I'm happy to carry on…'

'Esmoylda! Don't lie!' They all laughed as they went off to get cleaned up.

When they were ready to go, Drivel was nowhere to be seen.

'Doesn't he want to come?' asked Sarah. 'This could be the "big case that I can crack all on my own" [mimicking Drivel's voice] that he has been waiting for!'

'Ha ha. Of course!' said Stasia. 'I don't know where he is. I haven't seen him since he went off in a sulk because I asked him to help with sanding the staircase. He wanted to paint his room, instead.'

'I know!' said Sarah. 'But he wanted to paint it black, and I said no.'

'Well, he'll miss out, then. If this turns out to be something interesting, it will teach him not to sulk.'

'Esmoylda, don't lie!' they chorused. Including Esmoylda.

As they set off along the driveway to The Lodge, Sarah asked Esmoylda how Monty was.

'He's fine, thanks. But if that had been any other vehicle that Mudd was driving, I dread to think what would have happened. But one good thing has come out of it. We had a family meeting, and decided we are going to buck the trend of the Trolls' Code of Habitation... and all live together again!'

'That's fantastic!' exclaimed Stasia. 'I'm so pleased for you! How come you didn't say anything earlier?'

'I think because I still don't really believe it myself! It's sinking in slowly, and part of me thinks that if I say it out loud, it will jinx it. But when you asked about Monty, it seemed like the right time to say it out loud. Does that make any sense?'

'Of course it does,' said Sarah. 'Who would have thought that Arton Mudd would have accidentally made that happen for you? That he could actually do some good? I hate thinking that he got away with everything he did, though. I hope we don't have to have anything else to do with him. Hopefully, he'll realise that he had a lucky escape from being sent to prison, and turn over a new leaf. What do you think?'

Stasia and Esmoylda couldn't answer, they were laughing so much.

'Perhaps you're right,' agreed Sarah, smiling. 'But at least we don't have to see him again. Or Imperia Jobsworth. That is all done with, at least.'

Dorissa was waiting for them, at the front door to The Lodge. 'It's Imperia Jobsworth. About Arton Mudd!'

Chapter Twenty

The Face-Off

Inside The Lodge, Snooch was talking to Imperia Jobsworth. As they all entered the sitting room, they heard him say, 'So, who is Arton Mudd, again?' Sarah jumped in before Imperia exploded. 'How do you do, Miss Jobsworth? We haven't met. I'm Sarah, temporarily in charge of the agency. How are you feeling now, after your ordeal?'

That was like lighting the blue touch paper on a firework.

'After my ordeal?!! *After* my ordeal?!! You don't know what you are talking about! It's still going on! Worse than ever! No one believes me! Not those idiot Law Keepers! Not even my mother!'

The room fell silent. Snooch peered over the back of the sofa, to see if it was safe to come out. Everyone else was glued to the spot. Then Sarah walked towards Imperia and sat down beside her. 'I'm listening,' she said, calmly. 'Tell me what's been happening.'

Imperia Jobsworth at last had someone who would listen to her. And as she told Sarah everything that had been happening, quietly, and without shouting or crying, even she could tell that it sounded more believable. And, as she now discovered, as everyone else in the room had had dealings with the nasty side of Mudd before, it was easy for them to believe her. Each one of them in turn told her different bits of the terrible experience they had suffered at Mudd's hands. Except Snooch, who couldn't remember any of it.

'So you believe me, then?' Imperia was finding it hard to accept that anyone would.

'Yes,' said Sarah. 'And so will everyone else, if you are calm and consistent in what you say. And don't keep trying to justify yourself, and getting wound up. Just say what you have to say.'

Stasia and Esmoylda were most impressed by Sarah's wise words.

Dorissa made a note of them for future reference.

'Now,' said Sarah, 'if the Law Keepers aren't going to do anything about this, then we will. We'll go to him – he won't be expecting that. We might be able to catch him off-guard. Dorissa! Snooch! Go back to Koolton, and tell the Rizbers and Razbers that Arton Mudd is about to get arrested, so they had better keep their boys at home. Stasia – Esmoylda – you can go home if you like, as Imperia and I are going to have to face Mudd, and get him to show his true colours. And they won't be a pretty rainbow.'

'I'm coming too,' Esmoylda and Stasia said together.

'Don't expect any thanks,' said Imperia Jobsworth. 'I didn't ask you to come.'

Talking of true colours, Imperia's were starting to show again.

'Oh, we won't,' said Stasia. 'But we have our own reasons for wanting Mudd to face justice.'

'OK, but we'll need to be careful. Esmoylda, can you let your dad know what's happening? Tell him we'll be… where will we find Mudd, Imperia?'

'He's having a new development of houses built in Expatland, next to Blickly Manor. He'll probably be there.'

'That's where we'll be, then,' Sarah said.

*

Arton Mudd was in full flow, telling a group of potential tenants the advantages of renting a home from AM Properties, as he showed them around the new development. He was in his element, oozing charm while he mentally calculated how much money he would make. That was until someone from the back of the group called out: 'What happens if you struggle to make a payment on the rent, Mr Mudd?'

Mudd recognised Imperia's voice straight away. This was something he had definitely not been expecting. He tried to ignore the question, and carry on with his tour. But others in the group noticed that he hadn't answered, and they started asking the same question. Mudd was noticeably rattled.

'Yes,' called another voice from the back. 'Do you still employ Mr Garf and Mr Nostrils to sort that out for you?'

Mudd looked up and caught sight of Esmoylda as she finished the question. And at the same time, on hearing their names, Garf and Nostrils stepped out from one of the houses. Mudd told them to go back inside, but several of the group were now keen to know what this was all about, and told them to stay where they were. At a nudge from Sarah, Imperia Jobsworth stepped forward to the front of the group and faced the smooth-talking, scar-faced goblin that she had been living in fear of.

'I thought it might be best to clear a few things up before anyone signed contracts for these properties, Mr Mudd. You wouldn't want there to be any misunderstandings, would you? I have heard that these two gentlemen are employed by you to make sure that payments are made if anyone falls behind with the rent. And that it is easy to fall behind because the rents are extortionately high. But that nobody knows that until after they have signed the contract. Have I got that right? I'm sure you would want your tenants to be aware of all the details, wouldn't you? And, by the way, how did you so cleverly manage to steal my kattles, and where are they now?'

'Ah, we did that,' said Nostrils.

'Yeah,' said Garf, 'it was clever, wasn't it! They're in that shed, over there.'

'You imbeciles!!!' yelled Mudd. 'Get out of here, and send Riz and Raz to me. *Now!'*

'I think you might find that they are not coming out to play, today, Mr Mudd,' said Imperia, calmly.

'She's right, you know, Boss. Their mums rang in earlier to say they wouldn't be in today.' Garf was pleased to be the one to convey the message. It made him feel important.

'You've got *us*, though, Boss,' said Nostrils, not to be outdone.

Mudd turned his full attention on Imperia, forgetting that there was anyone else listening. He grabbed her arms, shook her, and brought his face so close to hers that she was almost overwhelmed by his rancid breath.

'How *dare* you interfere with my business, you insignificant little ELF! Your pathetic attempt to intimidate me just shows how stupid you really are! You can't say I haven't warned you. I can run rings round you - I proved that in court. No one believed a word you said when I had finished with you. But I can do much worse than that. I will make your life a complete and utter misery, and I will enjoy every minute.'

At that point, he was distracted by the sound of paper tearing, as every potential tenant tore up their contract. This made him even more angry, that Imperia Jobsworth had not only shown him up in front of potential tenants, but now had lost him a lot of money. And goblins like money. Very much. And so, this money-loving, manipulative, coercive-controlling, devious, lying, cheating, blackmailing, hostage-taking, law-breaking goblin was about to lose all control, and others (particularly Imperia Jobsworth) were about to get hurt...

Except then Clive arrived, and picked him up by the scruff of his neck.

'We meet again, Arton. Nice to see you,' said Esmoylda's dad, sarcastically, as Mudd dangled in the air, punching and kicking at nothing. 'Now, what shall we do with you this time? You seem to have a habit of either escaping, or getting around the law by intimidating the authorities. Maybe I should just drop you in the Stinking Swamp instead.'

'Very tempting,' said Imperia Jobsworth.

'But not necessary,' said the Law Keeper, who had just turned up, carrying a bowl of kattlefeed. 'Lucky I was in the area. And I witnessed the appalling behaviour of Mr Mudd towards Miss Jobsworth,'

'So did I,' cried Muriel, who had been out and about, helping the Law Keeper look for Lorry and Hardel. 'I'm so sorry, Imperia.'

'Have you got your prisoner cart with you?' Clive asked the LK. 'Only my hand is starting to ache.'

'Never go anywhere without it. Just drop him in there.'

Clive did as he was asked. From a great height.

'You'll be sorry for this!' Arton shouted to anyone who would listen. 'You've got nothing to charge me with. I haven't broken any laws!'

'Oh, no?' said the LK, strapping him in, then getting into the driving seat. 'Threatening behaviour? Coercive behaviour? Stalking? Taking money with menaces? We could start there…'

He set off down the road, saying:

'… hostage-taking is a good one… hit and run…'

'That's over… they didn't stick!'

'Ah but, Judge Peewit has retired, didn't you know? And the prosecutor has been replaced. It's a brave new world…' And then they were out of earshot.

The group of relieved-not-to-be-tenants were gathering around Imperia Jobsworth, to check that she was OK.

'Of course I'm alright. Don't touch me!'

'She's alright, then,' said Sarah.

'Apparently so,' Esmoylda agreed. 'Is that right, Dad, that there's a new judge and prosecutor?'

'Yes, I believe so. And they're not in Arton Mudd's pocket, so to speak. He might actually receive some justice, this time.'

Esmoylda went home with Clive, apologising for not going back with Sarah and Stasia to help with the sanding. Stasia said she thought Esmoylda and Clive had better things to do, like getting their family back together. Clive promised to come over with Esmoylda the following day.

Sarah and Stasia stayed a few more minutes, to watch Imperia and Muriel forcing Garf and Nostrils to open up the shed and give them Lorry and Hardel back. Once Imperia had the kattles, she handed them to Muriel, then turned on the goblins. She gave them such an earful, they couldn't get away from her quick enough.

Stasia wondered if Imperia was going to thank them for their help. But no. Muriel came over and said that Imperia said thank you, but they knew that she hadn't.

'Shame,' Sarah said to Stasia. 'It would be nice to think that the experience had made her a better person, and then it wouldn't have all been for nothing.'

'Mmm. Maybe it's a bit of an elf thing. Drivel is like that, isn't he?'

'I suppose so. Still, it's a shame. Talking of Drivel, we'd better get back and see if he has stopped sulking.'

☆

Back at The Gourds, Stasia scoured the house looking for Drivel, to tell him about all the excitement he'd missed. He wasn't in his room – and it hadn't been painted black. Rags ran through the house with her, looking for him, as she didn't seem to know where he was, either. He wasn't in the kitchen, or in the sitting room, the dining room, or the hall. So she ran up the long, shallow staircase, calling his name, until she heard a faint, familiar sound coming from the cupboard. Pulling the door open, Stasia was faced with an extremely disgruntled elf. Again.

'Perhaps we had better add this cupboard door to the list after all, Mum!' Stasia called as she descended the staircase, leaving Drivel complaining to himself on the landing.

'Ow!' cried Sarah, from downstairs. A sycamore seed had caught her right on the end of her nose this time. 'Flipping things!'

Stasia joined her just as Dorissa and Snooch arrived, and they all waited expectantly while Sarah read the message.

'Some children have gone missing from a dance school in Jettysville. The parents want help finding them.'

'Who would have thought that dancing was dangerous! That is scary. I hope they're OK.'

'But FG still isn't ready to take charge of the agency yet,' said Sarah. 'I can try and manage things from here, but I won't be able to go to Jettysville.'

'I could go with Esmoylda,' Stasia said, hopefully.

'You have to catch up on schoolwork,' said Sarah. 'You'll fall too far behind. And Esmoylda is trying to sort out things with her family, so I don't want to ask her. We'll have to turn it down...'

'No, no!' cried Dorissa, her hand in the air as high as it would possibly go. Snooch was copying her, although it was obvious to everyone he didn't know why.

'We'll do it! We'll do it!' Dorissa was squealing. 'We can go!'

'On your own?' Sarah looked horrified.

'I won't be on my own. I'll be with him!' Dorissa jerked her thumb towards her brother.

'I'm not sure he counts,' muttered Stasia.

'Yes, I do!' chimed in Snooch. 'One, two, three...'

'The message says that the dance school is run by a dragon!' said Sarah, and Dorissa shrank away, looking less enthusiastic all of a sudden. But Snooch shot his hand in the air again and shouted: 'Ooh, me! Me! Love dragons, we'll do it!'

Dorissa mouthed the word "dragon" to the room as a whole, her face distorted with fear.

'Thanks, you two,' said Sarah, pretending not to notice. 'I'll leave that in your capable hands, then. And although FG said she can't commit to taking over yet, I'm sure she'll be on hand for advice.'

'Great,' said Dorissa, sarcastically.

'Super,' said Snooch.

Acknowledgements

Kath Smith: for your calm professionalism and attention to detail in continuing to breathe life into The Sticks, while your lovely friendship and encouragement help to keep the story moving forward.
Katharine E Smith, Heddon Publishing @katharineesmith

Cat Clarke: for another wonderful cover design, continuing the beautiful vintage style.
Catherine Clarke Designs @catherineclarke_design

Lewis Palfrey: for sprinkling his digital magic on the illustrations, with some wonderful tweaking and enhancing trickery.
@lewisjpalfrey

Trevor Palfrey: for building a beautiful studio (along with cousin Richard), big enough to house 'The Sticks' family. For constant support and encouragement. And being head of the scanning department.

Ian Fennelly: for his on-line Urban Sketching course which inspired new dynamics in the

Wendy Newman: For her words of great wisdom once given to me, which I passed on to Sarah.

CPSIA information can be obtained
at www.ICGtesting.com
Printed in the USA
BVHW071107161121
621753BV00005B/149

9 781913 166533